Vampcirio

Acknowledgements

The author acknowledges the traditional custodians of Western Australia – past, present and future.

I thank the many helping hands to who without this book would not have occurred. My patient mentor, and author, P.J. Searle for his insights, inspirations, advice and encouragement. Thank you also to P.J. Searle for Vampcirio's wonderful book cover design. pjsearlebooks@gmail.com.
Linda Searle, thank you for the numerous readings, corrections, re-reading, and editing of my manuscript. My sister Jen Barizza, and brother-in law Paul Barizza, thank you for your readings, and suggestions of my manuscript.
Romantic novelist, Elizabeth Reed, thanks for your much welcome advice.
Katrina Weston, thank you for your reading of my manuscript. Kodi Weston, thank you for your insights into the game of basketball. All my family and friends thank you for your love and support. Thank you Megan Bosch for your prompt – *write about a Vampire who gives blood, instead of takes it.* That began my writing journey of Vampcirio. The staff at the Armadale Library thank you for your invaluable help. To the Armadale Writer's Group, thank you for your enduring fellowship.

K.A. Worthington

Vampcirio

2nd edition
Copyright: K.A. Worthington. 2021 2nd edition
ISBN: 978-0-6452345-2-7
Published by K.A. Worthington.

kwkarenaw885@gmail.com

Book cover layout and design by P J Searle.
Copyright 2021 pjsearlebooks@gmail.com

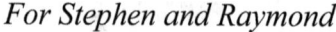

For Stephen and Raymond

ONE

He was just your average-looking Vampire. Standinzg at nearly seven feet tall, long gaunt, face, sunken cheeks, high forehead. His hair was pitch-black, and slicked back behind his ears, with a definite widows peak at his mid forehead. His fangs long and razor-sharp shone like the full moon when he smiled, and complemented his pale, thin, milky skin. He always donned the same black attire, long pencil-shaped trousers, black silk shirt, sporting a faux leather jacket, no cape. But he didn't have the usual Vampire traits. He could go out any time of the day or night and he didn't sleep in a coffin. He felt pain, joy, elation and devastation. Every three weeks Vampcirio Batt donated his blood. He had Haemochromatosis, but his HFE and ferritin statistics were at a good enough level to allow him to be a Therapeutic Venesection donor through the Red Cross Lifeblood

Donor Team. He had an abundance of the rich, red stuff to share.

People always shunned him when they saw him, they ran as fast as their legs would carry them, some screamed in horror. Children never ran away from him, they were intrigued by him, but as the children quizzically stepped closer to him their parent would grab the child and swiftly yank them away chastising: 'Don't you ever approach a stranger, especially one as strange as him.' The child would look back apologetically to Vampcirio, and fire an angry, confused look toward the parent.

Most of the staff knew him where he had his venesection. They welcomed him with a warm smile. They enquired of his well-being, and always ensured he was settled comfortably.

One morning nurse Sally was on roster to attend to Vampcirio. She was a spiritedly petite, attractive woman, about thirty something, with shoulder-length strawberry blonde hair, tied into a neat plait. She was the new kid on the block – the new Phlebotomist. She had been filled in on Vampcirio. 'He's not your average looking guy, but he is harmless.' Nurse Sally was informed by several staff members. After Vampcirio had settled himself on the patient bed, nurse Sally hooked him up, and gave him a small red squeeze ball. 'I hope I'm not being invasive, Vampcirio, but I'm curious. I'm always interested to know why people wear what they wear.' 'I am in mourning.' Vampcirio sadly stated. 'Oh, I'm so sorry Vam...' He interrupted: 'Oh no, no it's not what you think. I will always wear black until the human beings of this world treat the earth, all inhabitants, and each other with respect and kindness. I'll wear all the colours of the rainbow when the true colours of life are restored.' Vampcirio absentmindedly dropped the red squeeze ball.

Nurse Sally bent down to retrieve it. He caught a long glimpse of her creamy, silky neck. The carotid vein slightly protruded, as it gently pulsed. His eyes gleamed, and glistened, as he drooled in bliss. *'She has the most delicious neck.'* He lustily thought. Nurse Sally smiled sheepishly, as she handed Vampcirio the red squeeze ball. Her eyes locked onto his. She felt an electric warmth shudder through her body. Vampcirio felt his heart pumping wildly, as a shot of invisible light sprayed from his heart, and connected to her heart. Nurse Sally felt something in her heart region. A spark, a pleasant butterfly flutter. She immediately entwined with him.

Vampcirio didn't recognise what he was feeling. He had never felt anything like this before. He didn't want her blood, goodness knows he had more than enough of his own. He just had an urgent need to kiss that lovely neck, to totally ravage her with his – what? Was this love at first sight? 'I must control these feelings.' He dizzily thought. *'This has never happened to me before. I must control myself.'* Nurse Sally sternly thought to herself. *'This is terrible, feeling this way about a patient – not ethical at all.'* She tried all ways to rid herself of the alien feelings, but they would not subside. Vampcirio, and Sally were silently elated, as they parted ways, and took their thoughts and feelings with them.

Vampcirio lived in a large seven-bedroom house on the outskirts of Yanchep, Western Australia. Seven glorious acres, with several banksia, tuart, marri and stunted jarrah trees, crammed by nature on the property, that fed and housed a number of quenda, western grey kangaroos, black-gloved wallabies, Morgan cockatoos, blue wrens, short billed black cockatoos, and many an insect and lizard. In the Spring, exquisite wildflowers such as purple enamels, donkey orchids, spider orchids, Yanchep desert rose, cat paws, kangaroo paws, and numerous other wildflowers, mostly reared their pretty heads during September to November – the Spring season in the Southern Hemisphere – were in abundance on Vampcirio's property. Bull rush reed fringed a natural lake on the property. A natural cave, Cat's Eye Cave, was positioned to the east end of the property. It had seven natural sections. There were large spacious floors that presented natural pathways.

The Cat's Eye Cave was likened to a roomy non partitioned apartment which turned and twisted from the entry to the back. It sported a natural décor of exquisite limestone stalactites and stalagmites hanging from top and bottom, but never meeting each other. Each cave section had these stalactites and stalagmites, except for the first huge open-mouthed entry of the cave.

A full basketball oval on the property sat to the west, where Vampcirio loved to shoot the hoop. It was his way of keeping fit, and to shake off the grief most adults had caused him, through their nastiness.

It was a regular looking abode from the outside. Vampcirio's father, Vampyx, had brought the property in 1967, where he had transported the seven bedroom home from the planet Seventy-Seven, complete with the inside setup.

Vampyx, Vampcirio's father, looked like a real vampire, with the exception of pixie shaped ears, and he sported a pale orange complexion. He had a defined number seven birthmark on the nape of his neck. Vampyx had some Vampiric traits. He didn't need blood to survive, but would occasionally indulge himself with a bite of a human's neck to treat himself. The only exception being his life partner, Vivienne. He wore an elaborate cape encrusted with rubies around the collar. Tanzanite dotted the cape's flowing seams, and he dressed all in black. His flat, black, shiny shoes slightly turned up at the toes, and he walked with a regal gait. He could venture out into daylight for seven hours, but could go out all night if he chose to do so. He felt no need to sleep in a coffin.

TWO

Planet Seventy Seven was a wealthy planet where all sorts of gold, platinum, diamonds, gemstones, and riches were produced. Their ruler, Fairsevenite, looked like the rest of the population of planet Seventy-Seven. He had a larger gossamer wingspan that shimmered with all the colours of the rainbow, which set him apart from the rest of the inhabitants.

The environment was humid, yet cool. A number of gemstone trees dotted the planet, their petrified looking trunks insides were gem encrusted. If the trunks of the trees were sliced, a compacted gem pattern could be seen. The earth consisted of the seven colours of the rainbow. The medium sized rolling hills glistened with fine blades of emerald green grass.

The Seventy-Sevenites abodes were a domed shape, built from the abundance of Crysythyst that was mined from the natural mine on the planet, and used for varied structures and furniture.

The inhabitants were in the shape of the number seven, and were encrusted with precious metals and gems. They stood seven feet tall at maturity, had no feet, but could hover over the ground, up and down rockery, and up and down slopes. Any being who possessed the genes of Seventy-Sevenites could take anything they chose from the planet, but then no one could take anything else for seven days, until that object was reproduced by the Seventy-Sevenites, and replaced from where it was taken.

As one opened the front door of Vampyx's house, one was faced with a long hallway. One of the sumptuous sitting rooms to the left was furnished with a large crystal top table with its legs carved out of milky Crysythyst that was only sourced on the planet Seventy-Seven. Crysythyst came in an array of colours. The seven surrounding chairs upholstered with fine, lush olive green velvet. The frame of the chair and chair legs were carved out of clear Crysythyst, with flourishes carved intricately all over. Over by the wall to the south were seven, seven feet tall individual domed structures. One had a number of sports objects displayed in it, a football, tennis racket and ball, soccer ball, cricket bat and ball and the like. Two had an atom symbol with a non-flaming Bunsen burner in the middle of it. Three had a tree of life with figures of animals and humans entwined throughout the branches. Four had a Medical caduceus. Five had books, pens and writing implements. Six had mathematical symbols, and seven had different worlds in it. All the objects were inanimate, and consisted of pure gold. All seven edifices were in an individual alcove, side by side along the whole wall.

There were four bedrooms to the left and three bedrooms to the right. All the bed frames were brownish red Crysythyst, and had lace mosquito nets on pure gold frames that could be opened during the day and pulled shut at night. Each bedroom had its own walk-in wardrobe, with the main bedroom housing a powder room within the walk-in wardrobe.

The sumptuous kitchen had a double oven, a seven-burner stove, stacks of cupboards, a dishwasher, an island bench, double sinks and real gold taps. The bathroom was enormous, complete with a double shower, and spa, with authentic gold taps, and porcelain tiles, floor to top. The en-suite was double, with a therapeutic spa, a double powder room, two eighteenth century mirrors, and pure gold taps.

During the last two weeks – after his last blood donation – Vampcirio had nurse Sally on his mind. The more he tried to eliminate her from his thoughts, she just would not leave his heart. He had contemplated that the next time he saw her he would invite her for a home-cooked dinner. Maybe that was being a bit too forward. Maybe she would flatly refuse, or worse still, maybe she would tell him she was already in a relationship. Or maybe she would tell him she just didn't like him. What was he to do?

That night he dreamt of her. Although she was constantly on his mind – and cemented in his heart – he had never dreamt of her after their experience at the clinic, or not that he could recall any dreams of her. She looked so beautiful dressed in a pink twin set. Her strawberry blonde thick hair hugged around her cherubim face. She had a distinct angel-tuck in the middle of her chin. Her clear, icy blue almond shape eyes sparkled as she spoke. Nurse Sally sat on a high backed, leaf green Crysythyst chair, that had a soft velvety cushion, surrounded by a small group of five to six year old children, who sat on varied colours of Crysythyst chairs that had soft velvety cushions. She spoke in a soft lullaby tone. The children hung onto every word she uttered.

One of the children, Shila, suddenly looked very pale, and fell off her chair. She jerked and shook in a violent fit. In the midst of her fit she grew long sharp vampire teeth. He ears transformed into large, broad dog-ear shapes. Her hands formed sharp thumbs. Second fingers, third fingers, forth fingers and fifth fingers sprouted, all individually encased in a leather-looking segregated taut sheath. Thin-looking upper and lower arms formed, and her feet sported five long toes, with her legs being slim like her arms. Shila's face melted into a short, simple nose, with round beady eyes. She grew fine black fur over her body. Shila had transformed into a large, unusual bat- like creature.

The bat stretched out her enormous wings and swooped up and scooped up nurse Sally with her sharp thumb claws. Shila and nurse Sally plumed into an atom bomb mushroom of all colours, then disappeared. Vampcirio woke covered in cold sweat, and shaking. 'Don't take my beloved away. Don't take my beloved away from me.' He found himself screaming in extreme anguish. It took him some time to adjust himself to his surroundings. Although he had calmed down somewhat, he still felt he was trapped in his nightmare. Should he call the clinic to enquire about nurse Sally's well being? On second thought, *'No, they would think I'm crazy. It's only another week before I will see her.'* He decided at his next blood donation appointment, he would invite her out on a date.

Vampcirio's mother and father met when Vivienne was walking home one night from one of her meditation classes, back in 1979. Vivienne was not afraid of him when he suddenly appeared to her out of what seemed to be nowhere. She seemed to recognise him from somewhere, although she couldn't pinpoint from where. His first words to her were:

'Hello Vivienne, I'm Vampyx. I meant to catch you after class, but I turned and you were gone.' He wasn't really in class, but he had been watching her in secret, for some time.

Vampyx knew that she was the lady he wanted to be with. Vivienne was attracted to his deep rolling voice, and his hypnotic violet eyes, which she seemed to melt into.

Vampyx and Vivienne spoke often on their phones for seven weeks, before they arranged to meet at the local coffee shop. They hit it off from the start. Within seven weeks Vampyx had invited Vivienne over to his home for a meal. From there on, they were inseparable.

Seven months into their relationship, the pair moved in together at Vampyx's home at Yanchep, Western Australia.

Vampyx, was 70.7% vampire, with the rest of his genes being Pyxico, from the planet Pyxic, Vulcarnoaun, from the planet Vulcarnoau, and Seventy-Sevenite from the planet Seventy-Seven, all outside of the Earth's atmosphere. Vampyx had a very strong personality that equaled his physical strength. He was highly intuitive, caring, and empathetic to the way species lived their lives in their particular domain. He could make objective judgment without taking sides.

If there was a conflict between the planetary races, he was the mediator. Most times conflicts could be sorted out before a full-scale war took place. Vampyx was an intergalactic peacekeeper.

Vampyx could travel to the various planets whenever he was required. He would wrap his elaborate cape fully around himself, then transform into a shooting star. He could be there at the speed of light. He could then revert back to himself once he had landed on the planet of concern. After Vampyx had completed his mission, he would perform his cape routine and metamorphose himself back to a shooting star to arrive back to his partner Vivienne, and his home just outside of Yanchep, where he enjoyed his well-deserved family time.

Vampyx and Vivienne decided to set up a home. Vampyx assumed the surname of Vivienne's – Batt – as there were no records of Vampyx's existence on earth. Vampyx and Vivienne wrote their own their own special marriage vows. They committed to stay together for life, and celebrated their unique marriage by decorating their home together.

THREE

Vulcarnoau was about the size of Pluto. The planet had a green sun, and three burgundy moons. It bustled with the life of Vulcarnoaun beings. They where about two feet tall and string-bean looking. Bright orange-red skin shimmered, and pulled taut around their almond shaped faces. However they were stronger than the most stout weightlifter, and could indeed lift several tons – on their own. Their feet were like pogo sticks, and they would bounce up and down with ease whenever and wherever they trekked along their planet. They could balance very well when they stood in one spot. They were bald, with pin shaped dark blue eyes, and were a friendly race.

Their 'Queen', Tkobo, had violet almond-shaped eyes. This was the only physical distinction all Queens of Vulcarnoau possessed. Tkobo called a monthly meeting. She would gather the group together in an open space. The assembly had a spokesperson, who opened the meeting. She didn't have a panel of advisers, rather she asked the whole community for input into the betterment of the planet. Everyone was treated equal. There was no hierarchy. Tkobo's purpose was to gather the community together, hear their voice, and arrange to get done whatever was required at the time. A live vote was cast on any changes – the majority ruled. There were no qualms, as this was the way Vulcarmoau, and its inhabitants had forever functioned. All the community was healthy, and happy.

She preferred to be referred to as Tkobo, not Queen. She considered herself no better nor worse than anyone else. The needs of the community were fulfilled. The system worked.

Their medium sized, pyramid-shaped, huts were constructed out of Vulcarnoaumite, a rich, super strong substance that was hauled from the slow-running Vulc that ran a stream of lava from its top, down its side, and into a large caldera depression, in the Vulco desert. The Vulcarnoau people could shape the substance – before it set – into what was required, then cart the substance to its destination, already prepared for its purpose. Vulcarnoaumite, when extracted, for building, would set harder than granite within seconds. The Vulc was similar to a volcano, but somewhat different. Its soothing warm lava was full of therapeutic substances.

The Vulcarnoau races, and other universal entities could bathe in the lava to relax and rejuvenate. The bathers would self clean two minutes before their session ended in the Vulc. One could spend twenty minutes bathing in the Vulc, not a moment more, or the rich, supple substance would petrify them into an everlasting unconscious statue, forever encased in non-penetrable Vulcarnoaumite. This had happened to a handful of bathers over time. The unfortunates who had overindulged in the appealing lava a little too long, were given a Vulcarnoau funeral. They were placed in the Vulcaronic Crypt, where they would forever reside, with others who had suffered a similar plight. The icicle Vulcarnoaumite stalactites being their only company.

The Vulcaronic crypt stalactites were the only Vulcarnoaumite structure the Vulcarnoau peoples could not break, although water-wear had caused some stalactites to become thin and some had broken by themselves over millennia. One also had to careful not to be hit by Vulcarnoau rock, which at interim intervals, spewed out from the top of the volcanic like structure, but no one had been hit by the rock for decades.

Pyxic was the size of Mars. The planet had a purple sun and two pink moons. Their leaders Makopsko, male, and Makopska, female, inherited their leadership tiles from their parents. Leadership had been passed down throughout generations.

The planet had several food forests, an array of medicinal plants, and culinary vegetation sprouted within the food forests. There were many therapeutic hot springs dotted over the area. Six specific hospital caves were set up to attend the injuries of beings within and around the galaxies.

Hospital one was for the brain injured. Hospital two was for the broken-bone injured. Hospital three was for the heart and circulatory system injured. Hospital four was for the mind injured. Hospital five was for the drug and alcohol addicted. Hospital six was for the spinal injured. Pyxic's teacher of healing, Xiati was three millimetres taller than the inhabitants of Pyxic. She had a wealth of medicinal knowledge that had been passed down through the generations of her bloodline. Her teenage son, Treimix, was being schooled in the family's heritage.

Patients could only be bought to Pyxic via their individual personal guardians, who would appear to them in a dream. The guardian sought permission from the individuals' soul first, before taking them to the extraordinary healers on Pyxic. Some patients' souls did not feel the individual to be ready to further advance along their personal journey; others were ready to move forward. Those patients, who were ready to be healed, could be instantaneously healed. Patients would be taught how to manage their being and lives before they left a hospital. At times earthly doctors were baffled at how and why patients recovered from their health issues.

The inhabitants were petite six-centimetre pixie looking beings whose transparent golden wings would only appear when required for flight. No one could touch them, because of their fragile make-up. The Pyxico could touch other beings only where those beings required healing. They used their acute intuitiveness to determine where healing was required, then they applied the relevant treatments through touch and medicinal salves and herbs. They were sensitive, informed healers and carers, whose happiness lay in helping wounded beings to heal. However, those beings who required their treatment had to be bought to their planet to receive their help, as the Pyxico people could only survive within their own atmosphere.

There was no proof that Vampyx been born on earth, as he surely wasn't. Vampcirio's mother, Vivienne, and father, Vampyx never married, although they made a solemn commitment to each other to remain together for as long as Vivienne would live. That was the one and only time they spoke of Vivienne's mortality.

Vampyx could copulate with his partner, Vivienne for pure pleasure, which they had done several times. But he could not father an offspring in this way, even if it was with his lifetime human love Vivienne. Because of his heritage he could only father a child every seven years. The night had to be the thirty-first of October, just on the hour of midnight. Vivienne, being human, would usually need to be ovulating, if she were to copulate and fall pregnant with another male human being. Instead, all she needed to do was to be in agreement with Vampyx to have a child together.

Vivienne had to be taught how to set her mind to be in a fertile, conceivable frame. Vampyx naturally knew how to do this, since he was conceived in the very same way. Vivienne had attended numerous meditation classes over the years, and it was not difficult for her to set her mind onto one sole course, to become pregnant. It was the 28th of January 1982.

Vivienne and Vampyx sat opposite of each other clothed in their underwear. They clasped their outreached hands together, and gazed deeply into each other eyes. They both fully focused on the image of a baby; the sex of the baby didn't matter. Their thoughts synchronised and connected for several minuets. Although they were two individual beings, they had synced their mind and whole being together to become as one. They both saw a tiny baby suckling on Vivienne's breast. Holding this powerful thought for a few moments, they held their child between their chests. They both felt at peace and content. As they grounded themselves, they lovingly nodded and smiled in acceptance of each other, and accepted their child with gratitude.

Vampcirio was born in 1982, at this very home just outside of Yanchep, Western Australia, and yes, he did have a birth certificate, with 'father unknown' typed in that space on the birth certificate. He was born on the cusp of midnight, on the 31st of October. A full moon illuminated even brighter when he made his presence known to the world. In attendance was an aged African midwife, Mary, who migrated to Australia with her family in the late seventies. Vivienne was thirty-three when she gave birth to Vampcirio via a UNCS birth, where the umbilical cord is not clamped or cut, which gives the baby a continuing supply of nutrients from the placenta. It is believed by the alternative genre to prevent the baby from any trauma of being suddenly brought into the world, and to prevent the navel from being damaged. Thus the baby is thought to be non-traumatised by being gently weaned away from gestating in the uterus.

Upon birth, the baby is immediately given to the mother for an hour or so, while the carer(s) steps back to allow mother and child to bond. The placenta is wrapped in absorbent toweling, and placed in a bowl, next to the mother with baby attached to the cord and placenta, until the cubicle cord dies off between five to ten days. The baby receives continuous nourishment from the placenta.

The placenta is washed and salted every day, and allowed plenty of air circulation, to preserve it, until the process ends. Vampcirio remained attached to his umbilical cord and placenta for seven days, before the cord shriveled and died. Mary lovingly cared for Vivienne bringing her nourishing meals, and plenty of fluids. Vivienne, had unexpectedly learned of this type of birthing when she was on holiday in Africa in the mid seventies. At that time, she met Mary and her family. Vivienne had buried the placenta, north of the house, and placed a juvenile macadamia on top. The nut tree flourished and produced a bumper crop after seven years, and every year thereafter.

Vampyx was unknown to Vampcirio. Yes, his mother and father were a loving couple at one time, but his father had literally vanished into thin air a month before he was born. For some unknown reason Vampyx never returned home after his last mission. It devastated his mother, not knowing whether her beloved Vampyx was dead or alive, or even where he was. Vampcirio never spoke a word about his father to her, when they lived together, as he knew she carried a broken heart by the incident.

Mary, the midwife had filled him in as much as she could about his paternal father when Vampcirio was around seven years old, as Mary had met Vampyx several times before he forever vanished. Vampyx was extremely wealthy. Having had access to the planet Seventy-Sevens' wealth, Vivienne and Vampcirio would never want for any material thing for the rest of their lives. Vampcirio was an only child with no known relatives, only his mother Vivienne. Sadly, Vivienne had passed away in 2005, a year after Vampcirio had graduated with his degree in Sport, Exercise and Psychology from Murdoch University.

Although Vivienne had Haemochromatosis, there was no medical evidence for her cause of death, and nothing was suspicious. Vampcirio knew she died of a broken heart.

Vampyx lay obliviously happy in the warm, therapeutic lava of the Vulc. He had one minute to arise from his rejuvenation session, then he would return home to his very pregnant partner Vivienne.

He looked forward to hugging Vivienne, and to embrace her swollen belly to greet a fatherly 'Hello' to his unborn child. Vampyx smiled in anticipation at the thought of going home to his abode just outside of Yanchep, Western Australia.

Vampyx was in a translucent dream state, when he half opened his eyes. A large chunk of Vulcarnoaumite rock hurtled his way. He was still mostly in thought about Vivienne and their child. Before he could arise from the Vulc the rock thudded on the side of his temple. His head spun, he could see tiny stars, then blackness. It was twenty seconds over his allotted time to bath in the Vulc. The rich orange/red lava cracked, and crackled then hardened stronger than granite around his body, from top to toe, encasing him in an impenetrable coffin of Vulcarnoau. There he lay still, silent, unfeeling, but alive in death. The Vucarnoians were deeply grieved when they discovered Vampyx in his immortal state of stillness. They gave a short, sincere eulogy. They mourned, stopping every five minuets to salute the compass points of the universe, north, northeast, northwest, south, southeast, southwest, east and west. They carried him in his glazed, pale orange transparent coffin, to the cave of Vulcoaunic Crypt, where he was place along side the last being to which this unfortunate incident had occurred.

There had been no Intergalactic Peacekeeper for a few years. Seventy-Seven, Pyxic, and Vulcarnoau had lived in peace-their individual leaders had managed to keep minor qualms at bay there were no major discrepancies.

FOUR

Toungaur, the planet Krai-Qtaur's king, had a sinister smirk on his face, his yellow fish-shaped eye in the middle of his forehead glistened in devious delight. He saw an opportunity to seize power over planet Seventy-Seven, Vulcarnoau, and Pyxic.

Toungaur was born with a large a large KQ birthmark in the middle of his chest. This royal symbol told all the Krai-Qtaur inhabitants he was born a king, and he ruled with a tungsten rod.

When Toungaur heard the news of what had happened to Vampyx, he had tried to invade several peaceful planets. The planets' inhabitants were able to hold their own. Planet Seventy-Seven, Planet Vulcarnoau, and Planet Pyxic warded off the enemy. Krai-Qtauarians were multiplying at a rapid rate, while defensive resources on the peaceful planets were being produced at a slow rate.

Krai-Qtaur had a dull, medium-sized creamy/grey coloured sun, and two purplish/black bruised-looking colour moons – one moon being half the size of the other. It was a renegade world, always on the lookout to conquer the cosmos.

The planets' composition was that of muddy looking blue sand. Their abodes consisted of a part triangle, part oblong structure, high ceiling, with a solid dirt floor.

They were constructed out of Golair, a reasonably tough semi brick semi veneer mix of natural dark blue/black compounds, to the planet.

Wagjeta trees grew abundantly all over the surface. Most Krai-Qtaurians had varied sizes and variations of these trees growing in their front and back yards. All leaves of the Wagjeta tree were edible, with a variety of their leathery, flat dark green leaves being sweet, sour and savoury to taste.

None of the trees required water to survive, as they had their own inner resources to keep them alive. However, if the tree was uprooted, it could only be kept in its fresh state for a week. After that time, the arbour would shrivel, dry, and no nutrients would be left in the tree. The roots of the plant were inedible, but the inner part of their tough, Dynoectic feet, contained a dry, brownish/red coloured amber, Umberite, that was more powerful than dynamite. This substance could be extracted, via the Krai-Qtaurs' long, thin proboscis that protruded from the end of their thick arms, and sucked up into their wispy whisks, which acted as hands. After the proboscis had done its job, the safe cap at the end of the whisk shut, and opened only when in firing mode. The Umberite converted into a lethal substance via the inner workings of their whisks.

Their whisks being full of Umberite could fire at will. They could point their fully charged whisks in the direction of that they chose to destroy. A fully loaded, lethal nuclear/electric beam would penetrate their target, to where the recipient writhed and convulsed, and eventually plumed into fine puffs of green dust. The Krai-Qtaur were immune to sucking up plants destructive elements. However the plants' energy – if ever fired at anything, including each other – would destroy the receiver.

Krai-Qtaur beings were of a stocky, muscular, medium build, with a gunmetal shiny skin surface, although not the consistency of metal, more like the look of mica. The top of their skin had rows of fine fish scales, stronger than steel. Their two eyes – with a turquoise iris – at the sides just under their brows, and one larger eyeball – protruding in the middle of their forehead – were slightly tilted to the left hand side of their face. The larger eye sported a brilliant yellow iris set in the middle of a turquoise sclera.

Their heads were triangular in shape, and they had whisk-like hands that could dig through any surface rapidly, as well as fire Umberite at will. Their flat club-like feet sported three large balancing toes, with a trio of thick, wide-spaced steel like toenails.

They were a heinous race who thought themselves to be superior. They would allow no one or nothing to stand in their way of achieving their chosen goals.

Water of any kind was their only elemental enemy. If they ingested water, the fluid caused a rust-like cancer which ate the Krai-Qtaur from the inside out. Even a drop could cause the beginning of irreparable damage to the beings.

There was no water on planet Krai-Qtaur. Their lives depended on feeding on the Wagjeta tree leaves, and the use of Umberite. The Krai-Qtaur race could breathe any type of air, but their vegetation only survived with the planet's air.

On their planet, air was Kraiqtio, a unique gas pertinent to the planet Krai-Qtaur. The inhabitants commanded everything go their way. According to their way of thinking, they controlled everyone. All Krai-Qtaur were banned from entering Planet Seventy Seven, Planet Vulcarnoau and Planet Pyxic.

The Krai-Qtaur had previously conjured up many a plan to conquer these planets, and failed. If they could capture one planet at a time, they would have all the power in the galaxies to rule, and have complete power over beings. They would be the one and only to call the shots. Toungaur received the news from a Vulcarnoau spy that the planets were low on their protective resources. And yes, King Toungaur would make haste to take full advantage of the situation. On with plan one hundred and one.

FIVE

Today was the day. Although there was strata cloud in the sky, there shone brilliant, diamond sunshine in Vampcirio's heart. He was going to see his gorgeous, beloved Nurse Sally. There was a song in Vampcirio's heart and a skip in his step, as he made his way out of his vehicle. He greeted all at the blood clinic employees with a cheery 'Good morning.' As he entered the donation room she turned, and greeted him. 'Good morning Vampcirio.' 'Good morning, er um.' 'Nurse Charlotte.' The buxom young lady, with her natural plump lips smiled and extended her hand in greeting. Vampcirio had a puzzled look on his face. He felt his heart leaden. A queasy sensation wrenched inside his gut. 'You're probably wondering what happened to Nurse Sally.' Nurse Charlotte was a pleasant, good-looking young lady; she wasn't his Nurse Sally.

Nurse Charlotte could see his disappointment. 'Sally has moved on to further her studies. I'm her replacement.' Nurse Charlotte spoke in between gathering a few instruments in preparation for the blood transfusion. 'Now, let's get you settled.'

Vampcirio was a loner, but he never lived alone. He communicated with the wildlife that lived on his property, and enjoyed learning their way of living.

The dragonflies who made the fresh water lake on his property their home welcomed Vampcirio with their low hum. Their shimmery, translucent wings brushed past his face as they greeted him. The bobtail lizard poked out its tongue with a warm cheerio.

Every morning, he would greet his outdoor menagerie. Vampcirio spent an hour or so enquiring of their well being, listening to their woes, rejoicing in their victories. However, Vampcirio had one extraordinary, unique friend, his father Vampyx's special friend.

Acrobat was an exceptional Ghost Bat, a larger species of Macroderma gigas, Australia's false Vampire Bat. The only bat species in Australia to be carnivorous. Weighing one hundred and twenty five grams, with greyish/white fur and transparent, thin papery wings, she was first thought to be a he. She had lived well beyond her twenty year life span.

Mostly found in the Northern part of Australia, and Queensland, Vampyx had found her trapped in barbed wire not far from his property, just outside of Yanchep. Acrobat lay limp, and still, in silence, when Vampyx discovered her. She had a deep gouge to her underbelly; her wings were covered in bleeding scratches, her left wing broken. Vampyx always carried a set of protective gloves in his back pocket.

'You poor little fellow.' Vampyx said. With dexterity he freed Acrobat from her spiky prison.

Vampyx wrapped Acrobat inside his cape. He transformed into a shooting star – they were on their way to the healers on Pyxic.

The Pyxic healers stitched Acrobat's mangled wings with their invisible medical threads, and attended to her wounds with special salves that their forest produced. Acrobat's health rapidly improved. Her little gossamer coat belly grew bigger each day.

She was already a month pregnant when Vampyx discovered her. She made her home in the very back seventh section of the Cat's Eye Cave, where a couple of months later, in October, she gave birth to her first pup Persephone, as she hung upside down on a ridge in the Cats' Eye Cave.

The usual practice of female bats is they gather together in the nursery to birth their young. Acrobat was alone, with the exception of Vampyx checking in on her often. Acrobat was unique with her glow-in-the-dark wings, an after-effect of the healing with the Pyxico, and her long thirty-year life being attributed to the experience she had with the Pyxicos.

Acrobat

Turning Twisting

around she goes

skimming close to the ground

Stretches her translucent wings to the full

Twitches her large-lobed ears to and fro

Seeks out life

Her keen camera eyes

Zooms into a victim – a hopping mouse

'Yes, this one will do just fine.'

Hangs upside down, claw on cave shawl

her belly full of gore

Dreams of tomorrow night

she will bring her acrobatic skills to the fore

'Flesh, yes flesh, gimme more.'

The Cat's Eye cave had a secret section at its very end. It opened up its drowsy, relaxed eye after its daily slumber to a full shape of a cat's eye. It just as lazily closed its soft radiant eye at sunrise, repeating the process every evening, and morning.

Some of the limestone cave's stunning stalactites and stalagmites exhibited gravity-defying helictites that sprouted from the blunt ceiling stalactites. Coloured, striped folded fabric-looking shawls, as well as plain shawls draped from the walls and ceiling of the cave, while the cave's stalactite and stalagmite columns exhibited their clever attached weave. Thin looking straws, glistened from the roof.

The cave seemed like it was a magical world. Subterranean pools and streams scattered throughout the cave, along with the aquatic root mats from the tuart trees that dripped mineral-filled water, some into the pools and streams, that fed the abundant microscopic and macroscopic life that inhabited the cave.

Vampcirio visited Acrobat often, in the early evening, at her home in the Cat's Eye Cave. When she heard Vampcirio's footsteps approach nearer to the seventh section of the Cat's Eye Cave she would fly excitedly up to him. 'Chirp! Chirp! Chirp.' She would greet him with her loud high-pitched welcome, as she rushed toward him, her huge transparent wings stretched to their max. 'Hello, my little friend.' Vampcirio would say in delight, as he held out his arm for her to perch upside down on. Acrobat would sway side to side with her wings fluttering, in happiness.

'Chirp!' Hello my friend, how are you? How was your day today?' Acrobat always showed interest in how Vampcirio fared in his health, and in his daily activities. Vampcirio was always interested in Acrobat's well-being, and what she had been doing throughout her night.

Toungaur, the Krai-Qtaur king, gathered his troupe together, all 6061 of them.

'You, Sergeant, get the corporals together.' He bellowed. 'You, get those Wagjeta trees, and bags of fresh leaves inside the craft – like yesterday – get moving.' The Sergeants moved like lightning – some tripping over the other.

'Hey! Watch what cha doin.' One grunted.

'Hey tangle-foot, you watch it.' The other growled. The two Sergeants pointed their whisk toward each other. Toungaur was enraged, as he approached the pair.

'Save it.' He yelled. 'We need this fight for the real war.' He pointed his loaded whisk at one Sergeant, then the other: 'Unless you want to begin with two casualties right now.' The two Sergeants scowled toward eachother, as they crept away in silence.

The troupe protruded their slimy, slim proboscis from their whisk arms, sucking up electrifying Wagjeta energy from the root of the plant. They had enough energy to destroy the whole universe, if they chose to. But first focus is first. They could not afford any mistakes what so ever. Planet Seventy-Seven will be their first they would capture, then the whole universe – planet by planet.

Vampcirio was heartbroken when he left the blood donation clinic. His beloved nurse Sally was gone. *'Did I scare her away? Probably.'* He cynically thought. *'Why could she not tell me she was moving away? Why did she just up and go, without any*

indication? She must have known she was going to leave?' Vampcirio folded his arms. He was angry, frustrated. He felt worthless. He pursed his lips, almost biting through his bottom lip with his fangs. His eyebrows furrowed. He was bewildered, sad, fuming all at the same time.

Vampcirio decided he needed to take a brisk walk, try and wrap his head around the 'Whys.' He left his VQ7-Vehicle in the car park of the clinic, and began to walk briskly toward the town. His VQ7-Vehicle was one of a kind. It was dark purple, with a long, slender tapering body. The drivers side door could be flipped backward to access the spacious driver's, and passengers' bench seats. The dashboard was round, and displayed a series of symbols, that only Vampcirio could decipher, for driver information. Small to medium-sized gems encrusted well-defined V-shaped fins that adorned the front and rear, smaller at the front of the vehicle, and larger in the mid-section of the car. The mid-side fins acted as wings.

Whenever he chose to take a flight of fancy the fins opened up like wings, when the vehicle was put into flight mode, then after the joy ride was done, the fins retracted to become part of the regular car's body, after he landed back on the ground.

Vampcirio only used his original VQ7-Vehicle when there was no one around, most usually when most human beings were asleep at night, or around his property where no one could see his original vehicle zooming around. The VQ7-Vehicle could transform itself into any model car, or light air plane – and fly only as high as a light air plane. Whenever he chose to drive/fly when there were no people around, he did so in delight. The number plate on Vampcirio's vehicle read 'Vamps7.' That always remained the same, whether he was secretly driving or not.

SIX

The wind was mild as it puffed a slight chill in the air. The sun peeked out through the wispy, thin lines of the scattered cloud. Nearing the main centre of Joondalup, Vampcirio spotted little Timmy Benson across the road. He remembered the six-year-old child. A couple of months ago, Timmy had approached him in town. Before he could say 'Hello', Timmy's mother had whisked the child away. She had chastised the child, and warned him not to approach nor speak with Vampcirio. The child protested, but his mother was firm with her assumption that Vampcirio was a 'bad' person.

On this day Timmy was alone. Vampcirio had a devious thought. He would entice Timmy over to him, and lure the child to his home. He would mold the child to become an unpretentious, strong caring adult. He would find the child's natural super strengths, and work on developing those strengths to their full. At least that would be a beginning – one less nasty, prejudiced human being in the world, he thought. Vampcirio was about to call Timmy over to him, when Timmy waved in Vampcirio's direction. The child raced across the road, broadly smiling, and calling Vampcirio's name.

A red ute appeared from nowhere – Screech!

Vampcirio shot to where the child was in the middle of the road. His body covered the child like a blanket. Bang! Crunch!

Jerry, the shaky – white-as-a-ghost faced – driver of the ute raced over to Vampcirio and the child.

'Are you OK, man?' Jerry rattled. Vampcirio arose – dazed, and shaky.

'J-just a couple of scratches.' Vampcirio brushed down his clothes. He had skinned his knees. The palms of his hands were scraped, his knuckles a little gouged. There was a bleeding surface wound on the left hand side of his forehead.

A startled Timmy started to wail. Timmy's father, Lyle, raced over to the scene and snatched up Timmy.

'I-I-I'm sorry.' Jerry shook his head, still stunned by the accident. 'They just came out of nowhere.' Lyle clasped Timmy close to him. He gave Jerry a blank look, and Vampcirio a crooked smile, as he whisked Timmy away across to the opposite side of the street. Timmy's' mother, Janie, had seen what happened, and began to approach Vampcirio, then changed her mind. She ran quickly to join he husband and child. As she left the scene, she turned her head backwards, and mouthed a 'Thank you' to Vampcirio.

'Can I give you a lift any where.' Offered Jerry.

'No thank you.' Replied Vampcirio.

Vampcirio wandered toward his parked vehicle. He felt sick, guilty, angry at himself for what he had planned to do – kidnap Timmy. What was he thinking? He knew he would not physically harm the child – he was certainly no paedophile, but his actions, if they had been carried out, would have left a psychological imprint on the child's mind for the rest of his life. He knew his actions were a consequence of his hurt and dismay over finding out about Nurse Sally's departure. Regardless, he should never think about abducting a child – nor taking anyone away for that matter.

Vampcirio slumped behind the steering wheel of his car, sitting there for a long time without moving. Hot tears welled under eyelids, and tumbled down his cheeks. He cried and sighed until it felt though his heart would shatter in pieces – a lump in his throat – a lead ball in his gut.

Acrobat was due to give birth to her twelfth pup. She was thirty-three years of age, and had experienced the passing of a husband, and the loss of another. Her offspring had departed, and ventured out to create a life of their own. She had husbands from the moment she could breed, but she did not produce a pup every year.

Little Jym was born, weighing twenty-one grams, measuring five centimetres. Acrobat, with her fifty-five centimetre wing span, swiftly scooped him up. Baby Jym was born blind, with a darkish grey fur, much darker in colour than his mother's whitish underbelly and silver/blue topcoat. He immediately began to suckle from the nipple under Acrobat's armpit. Acrobat nursed Jym for seven weeks. After that time, he was old enough to be taught how to fly, and catch prey.

They had all night to Ghost Bat shop in the dense food-filled Yanchep National Park, and eat, before the Cat's Eye cave opening closed at dawn. They suspended themselves on a limestone rock fissure.

'There, there little son.' Acrobat shrieked when she saw a mouse hopping along the field. The mouse scampered along even faster when it heard the shriek.

Jym gazed in puzzlement at his mother.

'What, where?' He squeaked back.

'The mouse, son, the mouse! Watch what I do.' Acrobat swooped down from her rock crevice like lightning, and skimmed close to the ground. She spread her wings wide, all the while keeping her sharp eye on the mouse. She caught the vermin in her powerful claws, wrapped her wings around the furry creature, then bit the mouse several times around its head. She carried it back to their perch. They snacked on the mouse, and devoured almost every bit, dropping the tasteless head and feet of their dinner to the ground.

'There's another one.' Acrobat shrieked. 'Now you go and get it.'

Baby Jym alighted from the limestone rock fissure, while keeping his eye on the prize. He swooped down like his mother had taught him, caught the tiny mammal, held it down with his tiny claw thumb, and first bit the mouse on its belly. The mouse protested loudly, and almost got away. But little Jym, like a lightening flash bit the mouse several times

around its head. He bought the prize back to his
mother, and softly chirped with pride.

Jym had grown into a fine, robust young Ghost Bat
over the past nine months. It was July, the beginning
of the breeding season for Ghost Bats.

'Mother I need to venture out – go find a wife.'
Jym stretched his long delicate wings.

'Yes, son.' Acrobat agreed. 'You must continue
to increase our endangered species.'

Jym alighted from the Cats' Eye that evening just
after dusk. He flew northwards, remembering all the
things his mother had taught him to survive, including
to watch out for other bats, and birds who were
predators. He had taken the natural bush route from
his home, just outside of Yanchep, and had travelled
round 50 km of the 170 km toward Jurien Bay.

The night was a cold, at the beginning of July,
yet clear. A million stars peeked out of the low, dark
navy sky. The three quarter moon reflected its light
on the leaves of the acacia, tuart, and many trees that
landscaped the bush, like a thousand fairy lights. Jym
had to pause. He was famished, and exhausted
through flying such a long distance. He spotted a

lizard scampering along the ground below. Jym swooped down to his prey – swish! An object rushed past, then fanned its way down, up and across Jym's flight path.

'Whooo-oo-oof! Wooof! Oof!' Jym dodged and ducked. A medium-sized Barking Owl was after his supper, with little Jym being on its menu. The owl woooofed, glided, swirled, and twirled.

Jym dodged and ducked. He spread his wings wide to try to get up to a distant flight.

'One more time.' He encouraged himself. 'I have to fly for my life. Let's go Jymbo!'

'Woooof!' Jym felt himself being lifted up in the Barking Owl's sharp, small, hooked beak. Then he was dropped.

'Ooooof OooooH!' Being so excited, and looking forward to devouring Jym, the owl was not looking where it was going. He had lifted Jym a few centimetres from the ground, flew like a maniac forward, and smashed into a eucalyptus tree, just above the base.

Barking Owl lay on his back, displaying his streaked white and brown chest and belly feathers, in the salt and pepper dirt, its feathers bare in patches, its wing mangled.

'Please help me.' Barking Owl pleaded with Jym. 'I'm in a hurry.' Jym stretch his bruised wings, as he got ready to take flight. 'I'll die if you leave me.' Barking Owl wooofed almost silently.

'But you have the strength to eat me if I come near you.' Jym inched away even further.

'I promise I won't touch you. Whooo. Wooof.' Barking Owl promised. 'Wait there.' Jym just realised what he said. Of course Barking Owl couldn't do anything but wait. He was still flat on his back. 'Please don't go.' Barking Owl begged. Jym warily approached Barking Owl, and flipped him back onto his front.

'Can you move?' Jym asked as he backed away a little.

'No, I can't move a feather on this wing.' Barking Owl blinked his yellow saucer eyes, as he tried to flap his injured wing.

'I said I will not harm you. I am one to not go back on my word.'

'I promise I'll be back in a few moments.' Jym vowed.

Jym glided dexterously up to mid section of the very eucalyptus tree Barking Owl had had his mishap with, in search of a dead, strong branch. *This one will do.'* He said to himself, as he broke the rest of the half hanging branch from its bottom. Jym placed the branch next to Barking Owl. He gathered a mouthful of grass tree fronds, and placed that next to the branch. The branch needed a bit of work.

'Do you think you can gnaw at this branch, get it a tad shorter? Jym asked Barking Owl. 'I'll hold the other end down with my thumb.'

Together they made the branch into a sizeable splint.

'This will hurt a bit.' Jym warned as he stretched out Barking Owls' wing so as the splint could be aligned. Jym then wrapped the grass tree fronds several times around, and tied the fronds many times around the splint to secure it.

'Now I must be on my way.' Jym waved his wing toward Barking Owl, who stood lopsided near him

'Please can I impose on your help again?' Barking Owl spoke softly.

'I know.' Jym clicked. 'You're probably hungry after that ordeal. You were hungry before this happened, remember?'

'No, it's not that. I think I will perish if I'm left in this predicament. I appreciated you strapping my wing, but I am still unable to look after myself. I can't fly. Which means I can't catch my food, nor perch in a tree for safety. So you see I'll die out here on my own.'

Jym furrowed his brow, put his thumb wing on his chin in deep contemplation.

'I know you're bigger than me, but I am strong. See if you can hobble onto my back. You'll need to hold on tight to my under belly with your good wing, and secure yourself with your feet to me. Please don't dig your claws into me too much, as I want both of us to remain alive.' Jym suggested.

'First though I'll get you something to eat. I don't want you to be tempted!' Jym brought back a plump, tasty mouse and dropped it in front of Barking Owl. 'Cm'on, you have some.' Barking Owl invited Jym to eat with him. They both enjoyed their well-earned meal together.

Toungaur's army wore sashes of differing kinds. He wore a gold sash to indicate he was boss. The firing squad wore dark blue sashes to show they were the firing squad. The Sergeants wore olive green sashes to demonstrate their rank. The corporals displayed pink sashes.

Toungaur and his 6061 troupe back-loaded their three squat shaped Zymeryc space craft with their supplies. The Shape of the Zymeryc was deceiving. It looked much smaller on the outside, but it was spacious on the inside with a surrounding console for navigating the cosmos. The communication system split the console in half. The left and right of the console held an equal number of egg-shaped dials in various shades of green. Pale green for starting, lime green for taking off, olive green for slowing down, and emerald green for speeding up. A larger dark green egg-shaped dial was for an emergency landing. The dials illuminated once the craft was started.

The large grey, grimy looking, but clear screens took in the view of every angle outside of the craft. Smaller pale yellow screens monitored every space of the craft. The comfortable Z-shaped beds lined the walls of the craft. The crew took naps when their shift was complete.

Several Wagjeta trees could be imported and planted in the atmospherically-balanced terrain, situated in the midst of the craft. The huge KQ, the round Krai-Qtaur emblem blazed at the front of the craft. The army laddered onto their craft. Toungaur was the last to board the first craft, after he had instructed all the captains to check that the equipment was functioning to its peak performance, the autopilot set to Planet Seventy-Seven's destination.

'No. No. That's not going to work.' Jym twitched his thick protruding, claw-scratched nose. He was covered in blood pinpricks.

'I guess I'm just too heavy for you to carry.' Barking Owl wobbled on his feet.

'Now I've hurt my saviour.' Barking Owl blinked his big yellow eyes, and dipped his head apologetically.

'I'll stay here and look after you, until you are well.' Jym offered reluctantly.

'I'll tuck my hormones away until next year.'

'Thank you! Thank you!' Barking Owl enthused.

'I don't know how I can ever repay you for you kindness.'

'Just don't eat me when you get better. That payment is good enough for me.' Jym eyeballed Barking Owl for reassurance.

'Have you a name?' Jym asked Barking Owl.

'No, I am only known – by humans – as a Barking Owl because I hoot woooof, wooo whooof.

'I'll name you Dogfeather, of course if that's OK by you.' Jym beamed.

'That's very fine by me.' Dogfeather happily agreed.

'And you are?' 'Jym, but known by humans as a Ghost Bat.

The Kai-Qtaur were well on their way toward Planet Seventy Seven. Three, two, one. The first Zymeryc spacecraft skidded behind a giant cluster of Crysythyst. Vrooom! Another landed beside it, then the third bunked beside the second space craft.

'All well.' Blasted Toungaur's voice over the microphone to the inside of all three space craft. He saw the Crysythyst structure as an excellent hiding place, one where they could devise their plan to attack the Seventy-Sevenites with relative ease.

'All dis-embark carefully from your positions.' Toungaur instructed his troupe.

'File in beside me next to the mountainous part of this rock.' With all his troupe waiting to his left and right, Toungaur lifted his siliscope, similar to a telescope, but with a hundred times more visual power, and placed it to his forehead eye.

'There's a group of about 50 around a kilometre away, straight in front of us, all producing some precious thing.' Toungaur stated.

'Let's see if there are others around the perimeter.'

Toungaur spied a large group of about 80 Seventy-Sevenites to his left, none to his right, about 30 or so behind him. The Krai-Qataur were well camouflaged behind the Crysythyst.

'We'll attack in half an hour.' Toungaur stated.

'Those on the left of me, you tackle the thirty or so behind me. You on the right of me, go with me.' He ordered.

'What about the rest of 'em on this planet, sir?' One of the troupe asked.

Toungaur pointed his whisk arm toward the questioner, and zapped him dead.

'Anyone else got anything to say?' Toungaur glanced – condescending – around his troupe. The army shook its' heads in sombre denial.

Martyz stood at the back of the troupe. His eyes narrowed, his brow furrowed in anger. Toungaur Had killed Martyz's brother Zymtz.

'I'll get you for that, Toungaur.' He growled under his breath. Oh, how he despised that Toungaur weed.

Vampcirio lay in a leaden sleep that evening after his ordeal with Timmy, his family and Jerry. Although, Jerry, Lyle and Janie didn't bother him. Neither did Timmy for that matter, but it still vividly played on his mind that he had nearly kidnapped Timmy. He had just as vivid a dream that evening, but not about the traffic accident, nor about Timmy.

A smoky, swirling, shadowy figure appeared in his dry ice dream. Then the image sharpened. There stood a regal Vampyx, dressed in his finest suit.

'Vampcirio, I am your Father.' The sharp, strong, yet gentle voice relayed.

'FFFather?'

'Yes, now please listen very closely. I need you to do something very important for me, very crucial. Do you understand, son?' Vampyx was distressed.

'What is it I can do for you, Father?'

'There is serious trouble in the universe. One of the most precious planets, planet Seventy-Seven is about to be destroyed.' Vampyx continued.

'I need to show you what role I played while I was in this world.'

'I was an Intergalactic Peacekeeper, but since my absence, the Krai-Qtaur army – from the renegade Planet Krai-Qtaur – are about to attack the peaceful Planet Seventy-Seven.' Vampyx dipped his head in sorrow.

'There in the underground cellar inside the seventh room of the house is a cape of mine. It is black with 77 bright silver stars on it. This was my spare galactic travel cape. It hangs next to the smaller purple cape that has a silhouette of a full moon on it. Do not touch the smaller cape, as that cape serves a different purpose. I want you to take the cape with the stars on it with you to the north of the property, at midnight. When you wrap it around yourself, concentrate on where you choose to go. You do not need to 'see' planet Seventy-Seven, just concentrate very clearly on the words 'Planet Seventy-Seven.' Repeat until you feel yourself being lifted up. Do not be afraid, do not break your focus until you reach your destination. The energies will guide you there. I will be in your mind to guide you upon what to do once you reach you goal.' Vampyx took a breath.

'Do you understand son?'

'Yes Father.' Vampcirio nodded in the affirmative. 'But father, the door has never been opened, for I don't know how many years. Certainly it has been lock all my lifetime.' Vampcirio pointed out.

'The door will unlock when you approach it.' Vampyx assured his son.

The next day, mid-Saturday afternoon, there was a sharp rap-a-tap-tap on Vampcirio's door. Vampcirio opened the door, and was surprised to see Timmy, Lyle and Janie standing there. They offered Vampcirio a huge bunch of flowers, along with a large box of chocolates.

'I hope we're not imposing, mate.' Lyle extended his short, lean hand in greeting. Timmy ran and gave Vampcirio the biggest hug. Janie smiled her most friendliest, genuine smile, her dimples creased under both sides of her roundish cheeks. 'We just want to show our appreciation to you for saving our sons' life.' Lyle started to tear up. Vampcirio placed a contrite hand over his mouth, then quickly removed it.

'That's no problem.' He coughed, ashamed, between words.

'Won't you all come in – please.' Vampcirio gestured to the trio. Lyle produced a six-pack of beer. 'Do you drink mate?' He asked Vampcirio. 'Yes, just a little. Thank you.' Vampcirio lead them into his spacious kitchen, where the seven large, domed, ornamental structures graced the back wall. 'Please, make yourselves comfortable.' Vampcirio gestured to the Crysythyst chairs. 'I think we should have snacks with those drinks? I'll give you a hand, Vampcirio.' Janie offered. Vampcirio did not complain.

The 'friends' settled themselves in, and were soon chatting away like they had known each other forever. Throughout the conversations they had, Vampcirio discovered Janie, petite in stature with medium length blonde, wispy hair, was a school teacher, and Lyle, tall, but muscle toned, with light brown shoulder length thick hair, was a truck driver.

Timmy had wandered over to the inanimate structures. He was drawn to the one that displayed the sports gear. As soon as he touched the front the cabinet, in a split-second the basketball hazily exhibited a yellowish/orange three-second blinking glow, then dulled. 'Don't touch Mr Batt's things.' Janie, didn't see the glow chastised. Vampcirio saw what had happened with the structure, and he knew at once the child could be a star basketball player.

Timmy was a big kid for his age. Tall and lean. Standing at one hundred and twenty four centimetres, weighing around twenty-two kilograms. He looked older than his seven years of age, with his sandy, blonde, thick, surfie like hair, short, with a thin, wispy shoulder-length pigtail, cut to shape at either side of his head.

'We can sit out the back with Timmy, if that's OK? There's a basketball out there he can play with.' Vampcirio suggested.

'Please can we go out-back. Pleeaase.' Timmy begged his parents, his almond-shaped ocean-blue eyes widened in delight.

'Of course.' Lyle and Janie chimed together, as Lyle affectionately rubbed the top of Timmy's' head.

'We'll split up into two groups.' Toungaur stated. 'Sergeant Cryx, you're in charge of the 100 men you'll have in your squad. Go and annihilate the 30 or so pip-squeaks working at the back of us.' He ordered.

'Yes sir!' Cryx obliged without a protest.

'The rest of you go with me. We'll deal with the other germs in front of us.' He made an evil, snorting laughter noise.

'Sergeant Cryx's group make your way over to that big gem tree over there. Listen carefully to Sergeant Cryx when he orders you to do something.' Toungaur pointed slightly right. 'Yes sir.' Sergeant Cryx's team yelled. Toungaur pressed both his whisks down to quieten the din.

'The rest of you go with me over to the left there, just behind that contraption.' He indicated to the left of him.

'When I say fire, Toungaur motioned to his group of men, you, you and you do it.' He randomly pointed to three of his troupe.

'Only the next six of you fire, three seconds after the first three.' Toungaur selected the next six.

'Then when I call one two three the rest of us will blast all that's left.'

The 50 or so Seventy-Sevenites were honing a new defence resource – Nueconium. There was already a large crater upon which Diamise-Nuec was discovered – only two years previously – deep beneath the mid-section of the crater. No blasting was required, as the crater had been created by a meteorite that crashed onto the planet some two thousand years previously.

The Seventy-Sevenites' head scientist, Gemstarlea, and her technicians had created a contraption, known as a Quixinuec, that was similar to a nuclear reactor, and constructed within the surrounds of the crater.

Another post was set up to blast, and crush the ore type substance, Quixic that encased the Diamise-Nuec.

Diamise-Nuec was a rustic brown/apricot colour, and a combination of, similar to that in the human world, Uranium metal and diamond mineral. The contraption gave off no radiation, but produced steam, via a water basin hooked up to several cleaning pipes, that produced steam.

Part of Quixinuec's job was to fission the Diamise-Nuec, which was the nucleolus of Nueconium.

Steam was needed to thoroughly cleanse the processed Nueconium blocks. No debris could be left on the finished product, as would be rendered redundant if there were even the slightest speck of dirt left on it. The core of the Nueconium needed to be preserved in one piece. Instead of in the human world where, say diamonds are mined deep under the earth, and, for example, an open pit mining procedure is carried out, blasting needs to be done to break the ore. Then the ore is trucked to a primary ore crusher where the diamond extraction process begins. The Seventy-Sevenites' all in one Quixinuec, could carry out the whole job safely producing the pure Nueconium within a matter of minutes.

Connected to the Quinine, thick tube-like overhead implements carried the processed Diamise-Nuec blocks to several domed depositories where the Nueconium was stored in plenty. They were so proud of their chief Scientist and Technician, Gemstarlea, and her team for the invention of the Quixinuec.

Nueconium was the strongest, sturdiest substance, more powerful than nuclea, tougher than diamondsand was the Seventy-Sevenites newest artillery to ward off any potential enemy. The Seventy-Sevenites could catapult their artillery toward an enemy and destroy them with one swift motion.

Just after dusk, little Jym went about hunting for his and Dogfeather's meal. He had travelled round two kilometres. He was about to hang himself upside down on a ledge, when he spotted her, hanging upside down on a tuart tree branch, three trees away. She was looking closely to catch her meal. Jym approached the tuart tree.

'What are you doing hanging around here looking so gorgeous.' He winked.

Just then two more pairs of Ghost Bats approached the pair.

'Whose your new friend, Marnie?' Asked one of them.

'I er um...'

'Jym.' He quickly interjected. 'I'm just moseying along, looking for a meal.' Jym continued.

'We're all doin' the same thing – Terry.' He introduced himself, stretching out his wing, and extending his thumb in greeting. Jym reciprocated by hooking his wing thumb around Terry's.

'This is Kyla, and her husband Tyler, and my wife, Bessie. We're waiting on our friend, William. He's always slow to catch up.' Terry introduced the others. They all thumb greeted each other. Marnie thumb greeted Jym.

Vampcirio felt exhilarated, yet cautious, as he ventured toward the locked cellar within the seventh room. When he approached the elaborately carved oak door, it eerily unlocked, without him touching it. The light automatically switched on. He approached the two capes that hung side by side. He was very tempted to unhook the smaller purple cape, with the full silhouette moon on it, but he remembered his father stressing that he should not touch that particular cape at this time.

The room was surprisingly clean, considering no-one had been in it, other than his father, Vampyx, and that was years ago. It was 11.45, Vampcirio had 15 minutes to prepare for his unfamiliar journey into the unknown.

Toungaur motioned his men to approach the Quixinuec with caution. Crouching, ducking, and sliding they made their way behind the storage tanks, and hid about a meter from them. 'OK, you three men I mentioned earlier on, raise your whisks, and fire on that group just to the left of us. You can get a clear shot through this gap here.' Toungaur spoke quietly, as he pointed to the gap that bent slightly to the left.

'You other six, make your way round this building, and fire on that group in the middle there.' He motioned around the corner of the right hand storage unit.

'When I yell fire, you three fire. Three seconds later, you six fire. You all got that?'

The men nodded their triangular heads to affirm they clearly understood the instruction. Martyz half grinned, his mid-forehead eye glinted with hate, toward Toungaur, his mind filled with revenge, not toward the Seventy-Sevenites, but of what he would do to Toungaur when he was given a chance.

The Seventy-Sevenites were busily producing their artillery, oblivious of what was about to happen.

'Fire! Yelled Toungaur in his dry gravel voice. As the three men fired on the group of Seventy-Sevenites to the left of them, at the same time Martyz fired on Toungaur. Toungaur jumped out of the line of fire, and the ray of destruction hit the three quarter full Nueconium storage silo. There was a horrendous 'Booom!'

Vampcirio made his way to the north of the property. He waited for a few minutes, like he was waiting for further instructions, then he took three individual long deep breaths, in through his nose, holding for three seconds, and out through his mouth. He waited for three seconds upon exhaling before he inhaled the next breath of fresh air. Vampcirio felt a little more relaxed after these breathing exercises but he wasn't sure if he had even a slight shred of confidence. He wrapped his father's cloak around him and began to chant planet Seventy-Seven over and over again. Some time passed, when he felt his feet being lifted of the ground. He kept up the ritual. He felt his whole being floating around the cosmos. He was mindful that he couldn't break his chanting, so he continued on.

As Vampcirio approached planet Seventy-Seven, he passed through a stream of what he thought to be cosmic debris. A medium-sized, what appeared to be a meteorite, hurtled toward him. It came so close that it grazed his hand. 'Do not break your concentration', he told himself.

Vampcirio slid on to planet Seventy-Seven, on his belly. He composed himself, and looked around in disgust at his surroundings. Plumes of smoke swirled around, gathering momentum as it thickened at the bottom. Dust and dirt stung his eyes. There was metal and dirty rocks scattered around and the planet looked like it was only half a habitat.

'This is nothing to what I thought it would be.' Vampcirio muttered to himself. He couldn't believe his beautiful home, in Yanchep, was constructed out of such a hovel. He wasn't sure he was at the right place. He could see no life on the planet.

Vampcirio walked around trying to digest what this place was. Surely it was not the beautiful planet Seventy-Seven.

'Make your way over to that-er-um-pile of junk over there, Vampcirio.' He heard his father's voice clearly in his head.

'Surely this is not planet Seventy-Seven?' Vampcirio repeated to himself, as he shook his head in disbelief.

'It was, son. We got here a split second too late.' Vampyx sighed, his eyes cast down in despondence.

'Toungaur and his troupe had planned to destroy the Seventy-Sevenites who were working within and around the Quixinuec building, but it looks like things went wrong and they not only blew the Seventy-Sevenites away, but also themselves – and half the planet with them.

Vampcirio began to walk over to the Quixinuec rubbish tip. As he approached the junk pile, smoke billowed from the perimeter. In the centre of the pile was a glow of green, orange and red. Sparks of these colours in infrequent spasms spewed from the centre.

Nurse Sally was absorbed in her medical text. She was studying at the University of Western Australia, in the hope of becoming a doctor. This was her first year, with another four years of study to go. Having already completed her Bachelor Of Science (Nursing) degree, she had been accepted as a graduate into the Doctor Of Medicine studies. It was going on 11pm. She put her book down and headed off to bed. The day had been long indeed.

That night Sally dreamt of Vampcirio. There she saw a medium sized house, just a regular-looking abode from the outside. Children were sitting around laughing, drawing, and chatting in one of the rooms. Vampcirio came into the room to offer Sally and the children lunch in the dinning room. A delicious aroma of eggplant parmigiana wafted though the kitchen entrance, then snaked through the hallway down to the dining room. The children raced to the dining room, sat themselves down around the generous-sized Crysythyst table that was already neatly set up or lunch. Sally made here way over to the kitchen, where she gave Vampcirio a hand to prepare lunch. Did these children belong to her and Vampcirio? Sally woke at that moment – 3.30 in the morning. She recalled how Vampcirio and her had parted ways at the Blood Donation Clinic.

Perhaps she should have – ought to – contact him to explain she was moving on, and why.

'Perhaps not. I cannot afford to be distracted from my goal to become a doctor.' Sally reminded herself. She knew how she felt about Vampcirio. If she got involved with him, her goal would be diverted. She carried no animosity toward Vampcirio, but she had to let him go. Sally had to focus on her studies.

'Perhaps I'll talk it over with my parents', Sally thought. Sally's parents – Al, and Lani Coulston – lived in Fremantle, Western Australia. She was their only child.

SEVEN

Acrobat hung on a shawl ledge at the back of the seventh section of the Cats' Eye cave. It was a cool end-of-July early evening. She missed the company of her recent son, Jym, and she yearned for her husband who had long left this world, shortly after his twenty-year life span. She had twelve older children, but Jym was the only child she was aware of who was alive. Of course, she knew some of her children would have passed away due to their individual circumstances – there were always predators to be on the look out for.

A handful of her children could still have been alive, if they had not been caught in barbed wire – as she had been – caught by predators, or their environment destroyed by some human endeavour. Some could be feeding and breeding in their own thriving environments.

Acrobat and her second husband had – without intention – parted ways while they had travelled southward from the Northern Territory. Acrobat's husband had spotted a lizard scurrying along. He swooped to grasp the small reptile, grabbed it, and when he returned to the gravel crevice he and Acrobat rested in – she was gone.

He searched everywhere within and around the area they were in, but to no avail. He was unaware she was hanging on for her life, encased in the roll of razor sharp barbed wire.

It was just after dusk when Acrobat stretched out her luminous wings. The Cats' Eye cave opened its large elliptic-shaped eye. Acrobat flew out into the cold, clear evening. She had flown and perched for a couple of hours or so. She spotted another bat, who was about to catch a small mammal. The creature was scurrying for its life.

'This is one of my kind of bat. Not Jym though, this bat is bigger than him.' Acrobat said to herself.

Acrobat swooped down to take a closer look at the newbie. The newbie flew up with the catch, Acrobat flew up. They almost collided. They both alighted on a rock crevice, to which they hung upside down on. William, the newbie, extended his wing and stuck out his thumb in greeting.

'William.'

'Acrobat.' Acrobat reciprocated, linking her thumb with his. The two ghost bats were soon chirping away.

Acrobat told William that she had lost touch with her last husband, and that her son, Jym, had gone about his business of finding a wife. William listen intently, and conveyed his condolences upon Acrobat losing her husband. He listened intently as Acrobat told her story about how Vampyx had discovered her caught in the roll of razor-sharp barbed wire, and how he had taken her to the healers on the planet Pyxic.

'She is in fine form for her age – over thirty years old. Wow! She looks incredible, and she's single.' He thought how lucky he was.

The destruction on planet Seventy-Seven washed over the entire planet. The Krai-Qtaur army was almost wiped out, as steam from the burst pipes had got up their noses, stream washed over their bodies, and was eating their insides out. The group near the gem tree were blown into space, floating around like space junk. Toungaur and Martyz had been blown into space, but they were in one piece. Toungaur and Martyz found themselves sucked into the earth's galaxy, hurtling past the planets and pulled by gravity towards the earth.

They landed in the Gibson Desert, in the central east of Western Australia, about 1,324 kilometres north-east of Yanchep, the Gibson Desert being sandwiched between north of the Great Sandy Desert and south of the Great Victorian Desert.

They plummeted sideways on the leather, leaf-filled branches of a Desert Bloodwood tree, round 50 kilometres west of the Gary Highway, east of the Windy Corner side of the Windy Corner and Talawana Track, where both locations meet. The tree half uprooted itself through the force of the two landing so violently on it. It lay with its top flat on the ground, its bottom section partly embedded.

Blood red kino oozed from a gape in the mouth on the trunk of the tree, the sap having been there before the tree had been uprooted.

The kino sap of the Bloodwood tree was used by indigenous Australians, who lived in the desert, for the treatment of sore eyes, wounds and burns. The red dye of the Bloodwood tree was also used for tanning kangaroo skin water bags.

Toungaur fell from the tree and landed head first in the July mildly-warm twenty degrees reddish/brown gravelly sand, next to the tree. Martyz was next to fall, and sunk firmly feet first into the gritty sand. They were both stuck in the ground for a time, looking like a couple of bizarre stunted trees that didn't belong in this environment. Martyz wriggled, and wrenched. He freed himself from the tight ditch.

The wind had conjured up a dry, hot westerly that caused a flurry of low dust to swirl around in seconds, then almost die down just as quickly as it had begun. Martyz gazed around in awe at his surrounds. Spinifex mostly graced the parched terrain, along with a scattering of acacias, hakea and less gravelia. Gravelly rocks of all shapes and sizes were strewn everywhere. He tried to fire one of his whisked hand rays, it worked. Good, he still had a bit of power left in his whisk. He grudgingly looked over toward Toungaur.

'I should leave that piece of crap right there, exactly the way he is, forever.' Martyz muttered to himself. 'But I have a better idea, much, much better.'

Martyz left Toungaur upside down for a couple of minutes, then he pulled him out of his predicament by his short, fat, ankles, almost ripping his head off in the process. A nocturnal Greater Bilby poked its head out of its two-metre deep burrow in alarm, as it was rudely woken by the kerfuffle going on near its home. Its large, long ears drew back. It rapidly twitched its elongated nose – the whiskers on the end slightly shivered – as it peeked in astonishment at the two aliens The bilby decided to duck back into its burrow for safety and sleep. It was not time for it to wake up yet. Toungaur shook the rich, reddish/brownish dirt from his triangular head. He painfully held forth his twisted mangled whisks. He rocked, unbalanced from side to side on his feet.

'I've broken both my whisks.' Toungaur screeched.

'Well, Toungaur, you'll just have to stop smoking that funny stuff.....Siiirr.' Martyz snickered and smirked. Toungaur retaliated to the acid remark by pointing his whisks toward Martyz. 'Whirr. Click. Clack . Tick. Tick!' No fire. No work.

Vampcirio approached what was left of the Quixinuec with caution. Thick sulphur-smelling smoke still emitted from the perimeter of the junk heap, although the aroma was not caused by the S chemical. The air was polluted with micro debris floating at all heights from the ground up. The sky spewed the debris back down to the land. Macro junk piled itself up like numerous scattered anthills and knolls.

Vampcirio shook his head in dismay. Vampyxz sighed in sorrow inside of Vampcirio's head.

'Wait here for a while, son.' Vampyxz's voice spoke cerebral to Vampcirio. 'We'll need to time the sparks flying from this thing.'

Intermittent spurts of the green, orange and red sparks jumped from the centre of the Quixinuec rubble at two differing times. Every seven minutes a long spray of sparks ejected from the centre. There was a five-minute break, then a shorter spray spurted from the same area, another five-minute break, then the routine began again.

'OK, son, let's take a closer look at what's left of this thing. The middle of this crater might give us an idea as to how Toungaur and his army caused this devastation.'

Vampyx encouraged Vampcirio to move in for a closer look.

'We have five minutes to look, before this thing upchucks another lot of its dinner.' Vampyx concluded.

Vampcirio pinched his nose. He could smell something putrid, although there was no particular smell coming from the emission, only a slight metallic, dusty, earthy aroma.

Vampcirio stood on the edge of the crater and peered down at the boiling, bubbling substance below in the centre. The mixture appeared like some pretty-coloured dry brew, steeping in a cauldron, that swirled and stirred itself in slow motion – clockwise. It spat out bright, coloured, dry gas-like bubbles that rose, and danced from the soup. The top of small and medium-sized glass-like bubbles shimmered like green, orange and red tinsel.

The bubbles appeared wet, but they held no fluid, and emitted no dust when they burst. At every second the bubbles grew large by a speck of a centimetre.

'So that's how these sparks work.' Thought Vampcirio. 'The bubbles grow to their capacity, then burst. The bubbles must burst when they nearly reach the top, and give off their shiny sparks after they burst occurs, then emit that peculiar smell after each rupture.'

Surrounding the edge of the crater were tiny sparkling five centimetre objects that looked like minute gems of all kinds of shapes and colours-clear, pink, red, yellow, orange, green.

'I must bring food to my injured friend, Dogfeather.' Jym spoke to his new-found wife, Marnie and friends.

'Dogfeather?' Queried Terry.

'Yes, my Barking Owl friend.'

'Owl? Don't you mean fiend?' The cauldron of bats all gasped in horror. Jym explained how he had met Dogfeather, and yes, Dogfeather was going to eat Jym for supper, but due to Dogfeathers' mishap......... So you see, he needs my care until he recovers.'

'And then he will thank you by devouring you.' Terry frowned.

'No, no.' Jym assured Terry and the cauldron. 'He promised.....'

'I don't know about that.' Terry spoke with concern. 'I certainly wouldn't trust any predator of ours.' 'Well, I'll just have to wing it.' Jym stretched out his wings as far as they would go. 'I am not one to break my promises.'

'I'll keep you company.' Marnie firmly, but bashfully offered. Jym accepted, his sharp teeth glistened beach sand white as he smiled from ear to ear.

'I know of this cool, magical cave.' Acrobat conveyed excitedly to William.

'Oh.' William was not really interested in 'their' possible new abode, he was more interested in Acrobat. It was nearing dawn when Acrobat lead William back to her home to the Cats' Eye cave. There, hanging upside down on various shawl ledges was Terry, Bessie, Kyla and Tyler.

'William!' The cauldron was pleasantly surprised to see him. 'We wondered where you had got to.' Bessie sized up Acrobat in a friendly manner.

'This is my very good friend, Acrobat.' William introduced his new 'wife.' He went on to introduce Acrobat to the rest of the cauldron.

'Acrobat's son, Jym, told us about this cave. It certainly is amazing.' Tyler looked in awe around their surroundings.

'It's just what we need, and more' Kayla's eyes sparkled in delight.

'Where is that lad of mine?' Acrobat quizzed the group.

'He's some kilometres north of here nursing a Barking Owl.'

'Owl.' Acrobat widened her eyes in disbelief.

'Yes.' Terry pursed his lips in disgust.

'We couldn't believe it, and Marnie is with him.' Terry's bat nose twitched from left to right, as he shook his head in dismay. 'That owl fiend is going to have a double delight meal when it's recovered.

'But Jym said the owl has become a friend – heck, they even shared a meal together, and it promised never to harm Jym.' Bessie spoke hopefully.

'What about poor Marnie?' Tyla was concerned.

'I don't think it will attempt to harm Jym's wife – that is after it is aware Marnie is his wife.' Kyla tried to keep everyone's' spirits up.

'We should all go to Jym and Marnie – rescue them.' Terry nodded. 'He told us exactly where they are with that feathered fiend.'

The mid-morning was a warm twenty-five degrees in September. Toungaur huffed in defeat, as the fish scales on his belly and back rose and fell, like they were trying to catch their breath. He plonked himself on the red/ orange sand.

Martyz, unsure about this new, dry, yet plant-dotted environment wondered how it could support him. He had a little stash of Wagjeta in a pouch in his small back-pack. He retrieved some of the plant's leaves. The leaves were dried, dead, and had lost their nutrients. The crisps crumbled into rough small brown pieces when he picked them up. He had no idea how long he and Toungaur had been surfing the universe.

Martyz was starving. He had to eat something. He gazed bitterly over toward Toungaur, who sat dejected, mouth frowned, brow creased, a few meters away from him.

'No, I wouldn't even attempt to cannibalise him. The creep would probably poison me.' Martyz sighed in disgust.

Toungaur saw Martyz retrieve something from his back pack.

'Food?' Thought Toungaur. He was starving. Toungaur slowly made his way to Martyz

'May I please have something to eat.' Toungaur licked his lips with his rough, thick, black tongue. Martyz picked up a small gravel rock.

'Here, munch on this.' He shoved the rock between Toungaur's dense lips. Toungaur crunched the gravel rock between his dirty step-shaped teeth. It was an unfamiliar dusty taste he could not place. He almost blew the emancipated dry dust – as the Krai-Qtaur had no saliva – back at Martyz, then thought twice about doing so. He had no weapon to defend himself with, and besides he needed to eat something.

Toungaur bent to grasp another small rock with his teeth.

'Uh. Uh. Noooo.' Stressed Martyz, waving his whisk from side to side. 'That's all you're gettin' to eat Toungaur.'

Toungaur's mouth frowned, and his eyes blazed, as he turned to make his way back to his position.

'You stay right here where I can see you, Toungaur.' Martyz flicked his triangular head down.

'I don't want you sneaking any food where I can't see you.' This ritual went on for three days, Martyz eating dried Wagjeta with the occasional gravel rock. Toungaur was been given one small piece of gravel rock to eat per day. One mid evening

Martyz awoke to see Toungaur sneak a piece of gravel rock to eat.

'Put that down – right now!' Martyz ordered.

Toungaur seemed like he was going to throw the rock at Martyz, then he threw it hard in the opposite direction. Martyz raised his whisk toward Toungaur.

'If I catch you stealing meals again, I'll shoot you.' Martyz shot Toungaur an angry, serious look. Toungaur shook his triangular head.

'May I ask why you treat me so horribly?' Toungaur was puzzled. 'Don't you recall–you–you', Martyz couldn't think of another derogatory word to call Toungaur. The nastiest word around would be too good to call him.

'You murdered my brother.' Martyz yelled.

'Whaaat. When?' Toungaur was perplexed.

'Back before we went to annihilate that planet. Don't pretend you don't know what you did. I saw you, so did all the army.'

'I'm sorry, I didn't realise he was your brother.' Toungaur offered an insincere condolence.

'Don't you know your own army?' Martyz gave Toungaur a *surely you can't be that stupid* look. 'We have the same surname.'

'I only know my men by their first names.'

'OK, so who did you murder?'

'I-er-um don't recall.'

'That's because you don't give a Krai fart about any one but yourself. Isn't that right s-i-i-ir-r.' Toungaur, forlorn, sat.

Ten days passed. Toungaur felt as though one of his whisks had slightly mended. He dare not try to shoot Martyz, in case it didn't work. 'Martyz, sir.' Toungaur saluted Martyz. Martyz wryly smiled.

'May I wander over to that tree we fell onto. Just to check if there is anything beneficial on it for us – I mean, you, there? Maybe its leaves have dried, and would be more nutritious, more tastier to eat than this rock.' Martyz though that wasn't a bad idea.

'I'm going with you. Remember, don't try anything stupid. I'll keep my whisks firmly on you.' Martyz slightly raised his whisk toward Toungaur.

Upon Vampcirio's invitation, Janie Lyle and Timmy had become regular visitors. They often arrived with Timmy's nine-year-old cousin, Luke. They would all go out the back and shoot a few hoops together, then sit down to a sumptuous lunch. At one time Luke was curious about the seven inanimate structures. He fell into a hypnotic trance when he was drawn to the physics paraphernalia displayed in along the kitchen wall. No one was in the kitchen. He approached the structure, reached out and touched it. Vampcirio walked into the kitchen, as he was looking for Luke to join Timmy in shooting a few hoops before lunch.

The form with the physics objects turned around slowly in a clockwise direction for a few seconds, then stopped, and shone forth a red, yellow and green light. Luke was shunted out of his trance, and spun around. Vampcirio nodded his head in the affirmative. He knew Luke was destined to become a physicist.

'We're waiting for you to join us on the basketball court.'

The adults caught up with the latest local news. Vampcirio and Lyle had conversations about politics, although they did not always agree on various legislation.

Timmy was turning seven in a couple of weeks time, on October 31. Vampcirio had plenty of space where Timmy and his friends could scamper about. Although Timmy was an only child, he had a swag of cousins and friends, both male and female. Their ages ranged from four to fourteen. Janie, Lyle and Timmy were unaware it was Vampcirio's birthday on the same date as Timmy's. Vampcirio saw no particular reason to mention his birthday, as this was going to be Timmy's day.

'We will need to go back to Yanchep.'

Vampyx cerebrally spoke to Vampcirio.

'We'll need to act fast, as I don't know what this planet's destiny is.' Vampyx egged Vampcirio on to make the seventh bedroom. He was a meter away from the detailed carved door, when the lock unfastened. He entered the pristine clean room, and the light switched on.

Vampcirio's star cape unravelled itself from around his neck, slipped off from around his shoulders, and dropped to the floor.

The wardrobe opened up before he touched it. The moon cape unhooked itself from the hanger, and secured itself around Vampcirio.

'The moon cape has decided it needs to go with us – it has a mission to complete.'

Vampyx said. Vampcirio had a HUH? look on his face.

'You need to place the star cape over the top of the moon cape.' Vampyx encouraged Vampcirio. He did so.

Vampcirio was teleported – with his father Vampyx in mind – back to Planet Seventy-Seven. He landed unsteadily, but firmly on his feet. His head spun, as blood coursed through his body. It took him a few moments to compose himself. 'What we need to do is to go back over that puke hole on planet Seventy-Seven.' Vampyx spoke urgently.

Most of the bright five-centimetre gems that surrounded the perimeter of the crater had shed their brilliance. In place from their very tops, very fine gunmetal colour scales began to form on their body.

They had grown to twice their size since Vampcirio and Vampyx's swift departure and return. At the moment they were mere harmless, misshapen rocks – beginning to transform into a shape – that held no physical power.

'We must hurry, son. These fellows are starting to mutate into the very enemy that caused this devastation in the first place – the Krai-Qtaur!' Vampyx was uneasy.

'Take off the star cape Vampcirio.' Vampcirio obliged. 'Now, take off the moon cape. Start at the north of this crater, place the top edge of the cape there. Use one of those rocks to secure it in that place. Pick the shiniest gem that you can find.'

Vampcirio did as his father asked.

'Now pull the moon cape over to the west, and secure that post with another gem. 'I don't think it will go that far.' Said Vampcirio.

'Don't question, nor think about what the cape will or won't do, nor how it will do it, just do your part, son.'

To Vampcirio's surprise the cape stretched comfortably over to the west, to the south, and over to the east, each post secured with the four of the least dirtiest looking rocks Vampcirio could find, until the brewing crater and its surrounding infants were completely covered underneath the moon cape. The four gems that secured the four corners of the cape were left exposed, but alive.

The day had arrived – Timmy's seventh birthday. Much planning had been carried out over the last couple of days. Janie had nervously taken Vampcirio aside for a word about how the celebration of Timmy's party should take place. She did not want to offend him with what she was about to suggest. Vampcirio, sensing what Janie was about to ask, spoke first:

'I know Timmy's birthday is on Halloween. I really do not mind if you choose we set up a Halloween theme.' Janie smiled in relief.

'If the kids want to, they can dress in their themed costumes.' Vampcirio's grin broadened. His vampiric incisors glistened snow white. 'It should be a lot of fun. And I can just go as myself.' They laughed together.

The front section of the Cat's Eye cave was decked out with hundreds of fairy lights that entwined around mini jack-o'-lanterns. Some were turnips, and some were pumpkins. Vampcirio suggested the turnips, as they were the original jack-o'-lanterns based on the story of the Irish folklore tale of Stingy Jack, aka Jack Of The Lantern.

Stingy Jack was an evil drunkard who wandered about at night in Ireland. One evening he came across a body. The body had an ugly, ghoulish look etched on its face. The body was Satan, who had come to retrieve Jack's soul.

Jack implored Satan for one last request – to get sloshed – before he was to descend into hell. Satan took Jack to a bar where he transformed himself into a coin to pay for Jack's alcoholic drinks. Jack pocketed the coin next to a crucifix, which prevented

Satan from escaping. Jack bargained with Satan that he would set him free, if Satan would not take him for ten years. As ten years rolled by, Satan returned to take Jack to Hades.

Jack asked Satan if he could have one more request, to have an apple to eat, before he journeyed to hell. The devil once more agreed. Satan climbed the apple tree to gather the apple. While in the tree Jack surrounded the base with crosses. The devil once again found himself outwitted by Jack. Jack bargained with Satan again. In return for his freedom, Satan was never to take Jack to Hades. The devil was forced to agree. Finally, over the years Jack's alcoholism claimed his life.

Jack approached the pearly gates where St Peter refused him entry into heaven because of his deceitful, wicked ways throughout his life on earth. Jack then approached Hades, where Satan, remembering his bargain to never admit Jack into Hades, refused him entry. Satan gave Jack an ember inside a turnip, with a face carved into it, and sent Jack on his way back to the world. For all eternity Jack was deemed to roam the earth, with only a lighted turnip lamp.

Samhain was a festival in its own right. It honoured the end of the harvest, and to prepare for the winter months.

Samhain was from 31st October to 1st November, in the Northern Hemisphere. It was honoured between the 30th of April and 1st of May in the Southern Hemisphere. The festival pertained to the end of the harvest, and the beginning of the darker half of the year, winter. Bonfires were lit, the fire associated with the sun, believed to help eliminate the decay winter caused.

Prayers of protection were offered for the protection of livestock, individuals, and homes throughout the winter months. Food and drink were left outside one's front door. After these and other rituals, the celebrations began.

On Halloween, games such as apple bobbing were played. It is said at Halloween time, the veil of the Other World is most transparent, where spirits could easily approach the earth.

Over the centuries, fragments of Samhain, jack-o'-lanterns, trick and treat, All Saints Day, and other rituals were incorporated into Halloween.

The Celts brought their traditions of Halloween to America, where instead of a turnip being used for a jack-o'-lantern, pumpkins were used, as pumpkins grew in plenty in that country.

4.30 pm, children and their parents arrived in droves. They were dressed in an array of costumes – ghosts, zombies, nursery rhyme characters, Black bats and cats, and a few vampires were included in the mix – even a Dracula's bride.

There was food and drinks of all kinds. Spider web cotton candy, ghost bananas with chocolate button eyes and mouths, blood-dripping cupcakes, green, red, and orange drinks, a spooktacular cake castle with little creatures popping their heads out of the spidery windows, red toffee apples, and an array of themed goodies all displayed on a long table.

Vampcirio had invented a board game named Seven of Sevens. The board was numbered one – one hundred and five, with derivatives of a times table where the number seven could fit into the total amount. For example, 7x7=49. 7X15=105. There were three bags, which held various tokens. The first bag contained tokens, which read the sevens times seven co-ordinations. For example, 3x7= A player who receives a seven times token needed to guess the correct answer, being 21, then that player would move to 21. If a player incorrectly guessed the answer, that player would remain on the board position, and play was passed to the next player. Regardless of what number the player was on the board, that player would move to the correctly-guessed number on the board.

For example, the player is at number 21 position. That player has chosen a token, which states 6x7=? That player moves forward to 42. If a player is at number 77 on the board, and has picked 2x7=? The player must state the correct answer to the question, or move down to 14. However, if the player selects the token of 15x7=? that player would move onto number 105 on the board, provided that player answers the question right-that player wins the game.

Players were given seven seconds to guess the correct answer. No calculators were permitted, but a pencil and paper are OK to work out the answer. If a player was deemed to deliberately guess an answer wrong for the sake of not moving their token down, that player missed a turn in the next round, and remained at the position he or she was at the current round. The player who tried this method was deemed to be cheating by the majority votes of all the players.

For example, a 2x7 token was picked. That player answers twenty-one, the other players know that player should know the answer, but the player answer is incorrect. All other players cast a vote: 'He/She knows the answer.' If the player is genuine and does not know the answer, the other players keep quiet, and that player is not judged, but only misses their turn at the current play.

The second bag contained messages like: Miss a turn. Move onto 42. Move onto seven etc. (derivatives of sevens). Pick a treat from the treat bag. Go back three spaces. Give your turn to another player (of your choice). Give your treats to the player next to you (if you had accumulated treats). Take another player's treats. Choose a player to miss a turn. You have earned another turn. This bag also contained three Stingy Jack turnip lantern pictures. If a player accumulated all three lanterns, that player automatically moved onto 105 on the board, and wins the game. The third bag contained the treats. Players had a choice of which of the two playing bags they chose. However if the player picked the token that said 15x7=? that player would move onto number 105 on the board. If the player got the answer right, that player wins the game.

The game consisted of seven players, though less than seven players could play the game. Each player started by placing their heptagon coin on number seven on the board. Players voted for a leader who chooses a token from the 7x7 bag. The captain picks out a token, and reads out the question, for example: 7x4=? The first player who calls the correct answer begins the game. Subsequent players move in a clockwise direction.

Overall, the first player who reaches number 105 on the board, wins the game. The grand prize being a large unisex collectable Halloween themed doll, a scrumptious Halloween hamper – containing edible goodies – medium-sized Halloween dolls, a child's unisex costume and gift vouchers.

All were having fun. Children between ages seven and ten played the board game, and there were no cheats. Timmy didn't win first prize, but his nine-year old cousin Luke, who was dressed as a big bat, won.

There were a number of children on the basketball court, running around in all directions, and randomly shooting the hoops. Vampcirio made his way to the house. His arms were full of dirty dishes.

He off loaded the dishes, placed them in the dishwasher, then pressed the wash symbol. He paused on his way back to Timmy's birthday party, to watch the children running amok on the basketball court. He grinned at the chaotic spill.

Timmy had the ball in the goal area. He was about a meter away, on the left hand side, when he shot a perfect point. Vampcirio was pleased, Timmy being the age and height he was, evinced exceptional sporting skill.

Toungaur and Martyz were near on starving when Martyz gave his approval to Toungaur to approach the Bloodwood tree in search for some possible dry leaves to quell the hunger pangs of their rumbling bellies. Permission was granted to Toungaur, provided Martyz stood as a sentinel to keep a close eye on Toungaur's actions.

The strength of Toungaur's whisk grew a little stronger by the day. He knew not whether there were any Umberite substances contained therein, but knowing his hand was regaining some healing was a good start. Toungaur was pleased with this, but he had to not let Martyz know, nor give any hint. The air was arid.

The mid morning sun relentlessly beat the parched earth with its intense solar strength. Heat waves appeared in the distance, giving the illusion of shimmery, watery waves never breaking on the distant caravan of wispy vegetation, aloft the gravelly brown/red sand.

The Bloodwood tree looked fairly much the same as they had left it some two months ago. Toungaur and Martyz were just a few centimetres away from the roots of the tree. 'We'll search around the top first.' Martyz scanned the Bloodwood tree from bottom to top.

Martyz was about to take a step forward, with Toungaur in tow, when he spotted a Wagjeta tree in the far distance. The Wagjeta appeared majestic with its abundant, large life giving leaves. Martyz could not believe the miracle he was witnessing. A Wagjeta tree manifesting out of nowhere, and just at the right time, when he needed it most. While Martyz gazed in awe toward the Wagjeta tree, Toungaur took the opportunity to approach the roots of the Bloodwood tree.

'These roots should give me enough strength to terminate that piece of junk Martyz. Now whose the boss, eh?' He crept as close as he could, then tried to extend his proboscis.

Toungaur was overjoyed, it worked! He rushed over to the tree, and sucked up the substance of the Bloodwood tree root – water! He felt his brain start to seize up, his whisks began to rust, his legs turned into holey rust buckets, and he crashed to the ground.

Toungaur did not have the stamina to scream, rant nor rave. Martyz whipped back his head at the clatter of Toungaur's extinction. Martyz did not approach the dead Toungaur, instead he turned his attention back to the Wagjeta tree – it was gone.

'You fellows will need to leave us soon.' Acrobat cordially addressed William, Tyla, and Terry.

'Yes, we will leave tomorrow at dawn.' Terry replied. 'Our search for Jym and Marnie works in well at this time.' Acrobat, Kyla and Bessie were with pup. In around two months time they were due to give birth.

'Of course we will stay away until our pups are old enough to look after themselves.' Tyla interjected.

'What if Marnie and Jym aren't where they're suppose to be.' Bessie's eyes were wide with concern.

'We'll just wait and see, when we get there.' Terry encouraged. 'There's not much point in worry about something that might not be.'

Acrobat, Kyla and Bessie congregated together to ready themselves for their night venture. The Cat's Eye Cave unfolded its oval eye. Turning, twisting, frolicking around at the excitement of catching their evening meal, the lads left on their mission to free Jym and Marnie.

It was around eight pm when the Macroderma Giga men arrived at the location where Jym had told them he and Marnie had been nursing Dogfeather for the past two weeks. They arrived with caution, checking every noise, looking out for any possible predators. They arrived in safety, and gazed with suspicion around the area.

Three claw toe prints overlapped on the sand. What looked like scuffle indents were in one large patch about a meter from a lemon gum tree. Jym, Marnie and Dogfeather were nowhere to be seen.

Their worst fears seemed to have occurred.

'I told you that owl would devour Jym and Marnie.' Terry spoke with a low chirp.

'There are no feathers, no remains of Jym and Marnie.' Tyla scanned the prints and scuffle marks with his keen eyes. William peered around numerous trees. He flew up to a few in hope that Jym and Marnie had escaped. Nothing – no-one. They heard a distant hoot of an owl.

'Let's get out of here, before that monster comes back and eats us as well.' Terry motioned to Tyla and William to leave. They all took flight as quickly as they could, heading north.

A couple of weeks previous Dogfeather had recovered from his injury. Owls have a very high metabolism. When they are injured they usually only take around two or three weeks to recover. That is if their injury is not so severe that it won't heal.

'I am fully recovered now.' He came close to Jym. He made quick clicking noises with his beak in excitement, his large yellow eyes gleamed with delight. Jym took a clumsy step back, and fell over, as he and other ghost bats cannot master walking. Dogfeather lurched forward, and stretched out his healed wing. Jym closed his eyes. He could not escape. He surrendered and waited for his fate.

Marnie fluttered, and flapped. She shrieked in terror around Dogfeather, clipping him on the left hand side of his saucer yellow eye with her wing claw. Dogfeather brushed the ruby red pin drop of blood away from the corner of his eye, and blinked. He stared toward Marnie with a puzzled look on his face. Then he turned toward Jym. 'I sincerely thank you, my friend, for all your help.' Dogfeather enclosed Jym with both his wings. Jym was shaking, he was not cold.

'T-t-that's o-okay.' Jym's vampiric teeth chattered as he spoke. 'I s-s-suppose you are hungry?'

'I must bid you farewell my little friend.' Dogfeather woooo woofed sadly. Jym took a large gulp.

'I must find my family. They are probably wondering what has happened to me.'

Dogfeather gave Jym a mighty owl wing hug – with his right wing – then turned, and waved Jym goodbye with both his wings. Jym sucked in a breath of relief. He was saddened to part with Dogfeather, but he did not want to overstay with him in case Dogfeather was tempted to have Jym for supper.

Dogfeather had stuck to his word. He did not attempt to have Marnie for supper either.

'He's okay , for an owl.'' Jym's wing hugged Marnie.

The moon cape stretched like a snug blanket over the brewing crater. The cape bore a quarter moon when it had first been stretched over the ditch. It had begun to slowly move in a clockwise direction as it picked up the pace of its spiralling, and soaked up every scrap of debris from the ditch along its journey. As the cape picked up more and more rubbish, its moon grew to a half moon, then a three quarter moon. Then it stopped, like it was digesting the massive intake it had 'eaten.' Vampcirio was tempted to take a peak under the cape to see how it worked.

'Please do not touch the cape while it is doing its job.' Vampyx transmitted to Vampcirio.

'When will we know it is finished.' Vampcirio paced around impatiently. 'We won't know how long this process will take, son. A full moon will appear in place of the three quarter moon, when it has finished dining. On impulse it will fold itself up when it has completed its task.' Vampyx stated.

'We just need to be patient.'

The four posted gems, two shiny, and two half grimy had grown to 150 centimetres Their shape had changed, the grimy pair had partially transformed into miniature Krai-Qtaurians, the luminous part of them trying to form a seven. The two shiny gems were defining themselves as partial Seventy-Sevenites, their seven shapes a quarter formed.

Nurse Sally sat in the UWA cafeteria with her friend Blayne. She was in deep contemplation, and had hardly touched her lunch. 'Sally, Sally – Hello base to Nurse Sally, are you reading?' Blayne's call fragmented through Sally's occupied mind.

'Uh, oh, I'm sorry Blayne. What was that you said.'

'Never mind.'

Blayne scraped his chair closer to Sally.

'You've got that man of yours on your mind?' Blayne spoke, concerned.

'Yes.' Sally was peeved with herself. 'It doesn't matter where I am or what I do – he is just always with me. I don't know what to do.'

'Why not contact the man?'

'He might have forgotten me by now. What if he has another girl in his life. What if...'

'Stop right there, Sally. You're taking about what if.. He just might well be wondering about you. How you are, etc. 'But I left without a word. What if -.'

Blayne sighed, then interjected: 'Then again what if he doesn't? What ifs' are incidences that are totally imagined – they have not become a reality – might never become manifest. What if tugs at your brain, pulling the grey matter in opposite directions until your emotions are exhausted with worry-you begin to imagine the scene as if it is really happening, finally tying yourself into knots for nothing..' Blayne egged Sally on: 'Why not just find out? It will at the very least put your mind at rest.'

'I'll consider it.' Sally frowned, she was unsure.

'I had a word with mum and dad about Vampcirio – what I should do – they both agreed I need to consider my feelings, and my studies, but I am the one to make my own decision on what I am to do.

Timmy's seventh birthday party was due to close in 45 minutes. There was just enough time to play a couple of short games – and one unexpected trick was in store. Timmy's nine-year-old cousin Luke had wandered in curiosity toward the seventh section of the Cat's Eye Cave. Luke had a small torch with him that he switched on as the back sections of the cave became darker. He had finally reached the seventh section of the cave.

He saw a pair of luminous wings, wrapped around a fur body, shining nearly as brightly as his torch. Luke expelled a deafening scream. The thunderous noise woke Acrobat, and she shrieked in alarm at the sight of Luke, who stretched out his huge bat wings.

As Acrobat expanded her luminous, translucent wings, she flew in fury toward Luke's face, flapping her wings to protect herself. She scratched him firmly across his nose. Luke yelled in astonishment, waving his costumed bat wings to and fro, round and round, rapidly in a plight to protect himself.

Acrobat's high-pitched shrieks echoed around her home in the seventh section of the Cat's Eye Cave, reverberating off the walls. It pierced Luke's ears so loudly that he felt as though his eardrums would burst. He turned and tried to run, but he slipped on guano, and crashed face first into a pool of watered down bat's poo. Dripping with liquefied bat's poo, he raced as fast as he could back through the six sections of the Cat's Eye cave to where the party was wrapping up.

'Pheew, Lukey you smell like the dunny.' Luke's five-year-old cousin Olive screwed up her face in disgust.

'Come with me into the bathroom.' Vampcirio tutted as he took hold of the boy's hand. 'We'll get you pristine clean in no time.'

'The-there's some k-kind of m-m-monster at the end of the cave.' Luke stuttered, terrified, to Vampcirio, when they were in the bathroom. His eyes were wide as saucers.

'It had these big, bright things wrapped around its victim. It raged toward me. It screamed at me–and tried to rip my head off.' Luke's words jettisoned.. 'It was going to eat me next – it....'

'It was only a bat.' Vampcirio tried to reassure Luke. 'But...' 'It was your torch that shone on the bat. She got a fright from the light; bats don't like light. She thought you were an alien bat, dressed as you were. She had to protect herself as best as she could.' Vampcirio continued. 'Her name is Acrobat, she is my friend, and she is harmless. Bats do live in dark spaces in caves. They are shy creatures, and they certainly do not expect to encounter a human sized bat.' Luke had calmed down somewhat.

'I'll leave you to clean yourself up.' Vampcirio exited the bathroom.

Luke came out of the bathroom, pristine clean, sporting fresh clothes. Vampcirio rubbed ethanol into Luke's well washed wound, then he approached Luke's mother, Lillian. He explained what had happened to Luke and asked if Luke had ever received a tetanus shot.

'No.' Replied Lillian, concerned.

'He will need a tetanus injection and HRIG, Human Rabies Immunoglobulin, for immediate protection against lyssavirus.'

The formula contains antibodies from blood donors who have previously been vaccinated against ABLV, Australian Bat Lyssavirus. Although no known rabies-disease exists in Australia, lyssavirus.is a mortal rabies related disease that had extinguished the lives of three known people in Queensland, Australia, reportedly in 1996, 1998 and 2013. In 2013 two horses on the same Queensland property were diagnosed with ABLV.

The three human unfortunates developed fatal encephalitis and the two equally unfortunate equines displayed neurological signs, these horses were euthanased. Vampcirio didn't convey these fatalities to Lillian or Luke.

Luke broke out in a nervous sweat along the drive to Joondulup hospital. He fidgeted with his seat belt strap, as he sat in silence. His mother stood alongside of Vampcirio, as he explained the situation to the triage nurse. Luke was ushered into a small cubicle where a doctor checked him over, and confirmed Vampcirio's diagnosis.

Dr Haynes' assistant, Nurse Kane, administered the tetanus, the HRIG shot. Part of the HRIG was injected directly into Luke's wound, and the rest of the fluid spiked into the mid-section of his deltoid muscle. Acrobat's scratch across Luke's nose didn't require sutures.

When they returned to Vampcirio's home it was just heading into sunset, but there was still about an hour's sunlight left. Luke needed a HRIG injection for the next seven days, and he began a ABLV series of injection beginning that day, and continuing on once a week for four weeks.

Lillian was a sole mother who had nurtured her son from the day he was born. She was protective of him, without smothering the lad. She wanted Luke to develop to his full potential, in his own time, in his unique way.

Lillian thought of herself, as far as mothering Luke, to be there for him whenever he needed him, and she encouraged Luke to speak openly to her about anything of concern to him. She was like a guardian angel, always aware of her son's protection, as well as being a loving, nurturing mother.

Luke's father had deserted them when Lillian told him she was pregnant. Lillian had no idea why. She did not pursue him and he never contacted them. He had never seen his son. When Luke enquired as to who and where his father was, Lillian explained who he was, what had happened, but she did not know of his father's whereabouts. She held no grudges, although initially she was devastated when her ex absconded. If Luke chose to contact his father, Lillian would do all she could to help him.

Lillian was concerned for Luke's well being at this ABLV stage, as she loved her son, and Luke had only travelled a short distance along his life's path. Lillian and Luke had to wait at least for the next month for any potential ABLV symptoms to appear. When they arrived back at Vampcirio's home, Luke joined the other children on the basketball ground, the bat incident forgotten.

Martyz wandered haphazardly about in the Gibson Desert, his senses were somewhat fractured from the heat. His belly rumbled, his guts twisted in pain, in protest to his lack of real Wagjeta food. He had consumed the last of his small stash of overly dried, tasteless Wagjeta leaves a few days ago – or was that a few weeks. He was totally reliant on dusty, distasteful gravel rock for his meals. He was headed north, but did not comprehend what direction he had embarked toward.

Toungaur was gone. (Thank the Krai-Qtaur for small mercies) he thought. The day was coming to a close, but the air was still dry and hot. 'Where had that luscious Wagjeta tree gone?' He said to himself.

Martyz came across a pygmy mulga monitor, and a short-beaked echidna. A king brown snake's forked tongue tasted its way to him, its glassy, unblinking eyes never wavering from him. As its mouth opened wide it sprung forward – at lightning speed – and considered biting him, then it scuttled away, puzzled because it didn't recognise the species.

A large red kangaroo approached Martyz. It kept its steady, piercing, gaze on him, as it raised its to paws to a boxing challenge. The big red then decided to retreat. As it bounded away, it stared back toward Martyz in confusion, as if wondering what it was seeing.

Martyz thought he might be able to eat an animal he saw, but he soon found out they contain fluid when he threw a rock at a dingo who looked like it was going to attack him. This was enough to make the dog whimper and retreat. He only scratched the side of the dingo, when he saw red fluid on the surface of its wound. 'That thing bleeds like that tree Toungaur and I crashed into.' Martyz concluded.

The two grimy, dual Krai-Qutaur/sparkling Seventy-Sevenite gems began to grow dynamite whisks. Their hands were just beginning to protrude, like little mammary bumps. As the mounds grew, at intervals of their growth, they received an invisible charge of strength and vitality.

The four gems peeled away their outer skins – like the peeling of a banana – to reveal two sparkling Seventy-Sevens who grew some more, their seven shape, and shimmering gems become more prominent with each spurt of growth. Their appearance was a Seventy-Sevenite, with the exception that these two had grown two Krai-Qtaur whisks, that were empowered with a substance similar to Nuconium, that had been mined on planet Seventy-Seven. The two grimy gems followed suite. They embodied the Krai-Qtaur looks, but had grown sparkling gems from head to toe. These two curiosities were empowered with a substance similar to Umberite, the substance produced by the Wagjeta tree trunk.

The moon cape had almost completed its task. The moon was almost full in the mid section of the soft, vibrant, aqua, silk material.

One of the Curiosity Krai-Qtaur whisks was nearing maturity. It tilted the greyish, metallic, cagey arm in the direction of the glittery Curiosity Seventy-Sevenite – the one closest to it. It protruded its weapon, then protracted the weapon several times. Its Krai-Qtaur war mind was telling it to attack without mercy, but its peaceful Seventy-Sevenite heart was telling it to keep calm. Upon a protraction of its whisk, the Curiosity Krai-Qtaur accidentally threw a wavelet of new Umberite energy toward the unsuspecting Curiosity Seventy-Sevenite, who was farther from it. The shot missed. The annoyed Curiosity Seventy-Sevenite – who thought it was being targeted – folded itself in half, and emitted a great purplish cloud of laser dust. The accidental sharp shooter thought it had hit the unsuspecting Seventy-Sevenite. Its caring emotions took over, as it rushed to help the 'injured' one. The other Curiosity Krai-Qutaur, who looked from side-to-side – like it was supervising a wrestling match – took a step backward, and slipped over the edge of the dilapidated Quixinuec onto the edge of the moon cape, where it slid through into the Quixinuec's chasm. The 'helper' copped another bolt of purplish dust – this time it was bullseye.

Debris sprayed from the shattered Curiosity Krai-Qtaur, who had been dusted and busted. Some of the fine, shattered shards fell onto the moon cape. The cape turned itself inside out, and sucked up the splinters.

The moon cape had completed its job. It had overtaxed its own energy through the extra burden of chewing up the fallen Curiosity Krai-Qtaur, and clearing the debris of the exploded Curiosity Krai-Qtaur. The full moon on the cape was crumbling. At the same time, the moon shook and shivered in the middle of the cape, then without warning jumped off the cape-like it was on fire, and at lightning speed positioned itself in the sky above planet Seventy-Seven.

During the moon's transition, it left behind a colossus vortex of dusty, silvery, sparkly stardust. Some stardust magnetised together to form whole stars that spewed backward, forward, up, and down, until they glued themselves across the indigo sky. The cape itself folded up into a neat cylinder, rolled over to Vampcirio, and parked itself at his feet.

'Our work is complete here, son.' Vampyx scanned the terrain from all four corners.

Vampcirio, and Vampyx left planet Seventy-Seven. They teleported themselves back to their home at Yanchep. The star cape was in perfect condition. All of its stars – in all their positions – on the background of the royal blue material. The moon cape's material was in pristine condition, with the exception of its missing moon that was now the new moon in the galaxy of planet Seventy-Seven.

Vampyx could see Vampcirio's baffled look:

'The moon cape will take some time to rejuvenate. It has used up all its resources to complete its job. Vampyx frowned a little in contemplation: 'The moon cape may, or may not be used again. This task was the most colossal – most exhausting – it has ever done.' Vampyx emerged from Vampcirio's mind and stood like a holograph, reflected upon the moon-cape who had completed the task of producing a new moon for one of the smaller planets, but he could not recall the cape dealing with a structure such as the dilapidated Quixinuec – nor its contents, or its offspring, before this incident.

'What will happen to planet Seventy-Seven now, father?'

'I cannot say, son. Seventy-Seven has been traumatised, beyond trauma. The planet may or may not recover.' Vampyx shrugged with uncertainty.

The moon cape, and the star cape were placed back in their proper positions – inside the wardrobe – in the seventh room of the house.

'Now I must go. Farewell, my son.' Vampyx waved his right hand, as he departed.

'But father.....' Vampyx faded away, in degrees, until he disappeared.

Only two Seventy-Sevenites were left in the whole existence of their planet – and they were not 'purely' original – one female, and one male.

Lightshim and Lightsher gazed in downhearted wonder around their home. All putrid odours and heavy fog from the Quixinuec blast had cleared. There in front of them stood the deep void of the now useless Quixinuec – not one sound, not one tremor.

Tons of chunky piles of small, medium and large burnt coal-like debris – the aftermath of the massive explosion – were stacked, packed, and trailed all over the immediate vicinity. The mess could be seen as far as the eye stretched.

Lightsher, and Lightshim's mind boggled at the sight. *Where should we begin re-building? And with what?* They looked forlorn toward each other.

'We cannot build our home, even a simple, comfortable one – with this – the resources this rubbish-tip has on offer.' They both spoke to each other in unison.

Would there be time for breeding? Who knew? The pair of Seventy-Sevenites, sighed despondent. Tears stung their eyes, streamed down their faces as their hearts broke, and splintered. Their mid-sections shuddered, shook with their grief. Jewel tears from their eyes flowed forth like a rapid miniature waterfall. Small pools of liquefied diamonds, sapphires, rubies and other gems formed tiny rainbow streams that shimmied along, then with a rapid rush meandered north, southeast, and west. Small ponds pooled on the parched, ugly ground. Four slimline strips of water stemmed from the four compass points, rushed to the mid section of the ground, stopped, then pooled together to create a larger pond in the mid-section of the area.

It was nearing the end of October, when Acrobat gave birth to a healthy baby girl, Gillian. Bessie followed suit within a couple of days. She birthed a robust son, Liam. Kyla produced a small, but fit girl, Jennifer, a few hours after Bessie. The mothers helped each other in gathering food and bat-sitting each other's babies. When Bessie was unwell one evening, Acrobat and Kyla provided food and comfort to her.

Terry, William and Tyla winged from the Cat's Eye cave in Yanchep at dusk and headed north, then they wheeled east of the Great Northern Highway.

They air travelled around 700 kilometres to Sandstone, stopping for sleeps during the days and eats during the evenings along the way.

They air-trekked a further 150 kilometres to Leinster, stopping for breaks, then moved on around another 90 kilometres slightly north to arrive at the Wanjarri National Park. The sun had dipped on the horizon an hour previously and had closed its dial for the day. The moon was in its final quarter and appeared to be a luminous croissant in the dark, star-specked sky. The three friends spotted an old Eucalyptus Camaldulensis, about 30 metres high, its pale brown scaly bark had an ancient hollow down the bottom of its trunk, about a half a metre up from the tree roots.

A juvenile Gould's Wattled Bat peeked out of the well-aged hollow. Terry, William and Tyler swiftly descended to the area. The juvenile bat shyly emerged out of the tree hollow and seemed confused about its surroundings.

Terry, William and Tyla stood their ground, as the tiny creature scraped itself toward them.

'I don't know where I am. I'm lost' Cried the junior bat. 'How on earth did you do that?' Asked Tyler.

'I don't know. I flew out to gather some dinner last night, or was the night before. I don't recall.' The distressed mammal continued. 'I had plenty to eat, but then I couldn't remember which way I had flown from my home, nor in which direction. So I just kept on flying, and stopping for a day's rest and a night's hunt, in the hope of reaching my home.' The juvenile took a despondent, long sigh. 'I don't know how long I have been away from my home, but I miss my family.'

'Do you have any idea, even the slightest notion, where the direction of your home could be?' Tyla enquired.

'It's somewhere up there;' the youngster pointed north, paused for a moment in perplexed thought. 'Or maybe over there.' He thumb pointed to the east.

'We can try to help you find you way home.' Terry suggested, 'But I don't like our chances of doing that, if you are unsure of where your abode lies.

'We're heading up to the Kimberly. I suppose we can make a change in our route. Please try to remember a little, that way we can try and get you back home.'

'Oh, thank you! Thank you!' The youngster enthused. 'My name is Gerry.' He held his tiny thumb forth in greeting.

Terry, William and Tyla reciprocated.

'I think we can make a start here.' Gerry pointed north-east, although he wasn't exactly sure, but said nothing else.

NINE

Nurse Sally half-halfheartedly decided to try to make contact with Vampcirio. The *'What Ifs'* wrung out their persistent, darkest powers into her mind, but she managed to reign in those pessimistic notions so as they would not sabotage her complete purpose. She remembered the advice her good friend Blayne had conveyed, *'What Ifs' are non tangible assumptions – it may never happen.'*

She didn't want to contact the hospital by phone to obtain Vampcirio's personal details – particularly where he lived – if he had moved from his previous address. She was willing to approach the hospital to ask when Vampcirio was due for his next blood donation, that is if indeed he still contributed. She didn't want to go to the hospital alone, so she asked her friend, Blayne, if he would accompany her. He was happy to do so, and obliged.

Blayne and Sally pulled up at the west end of Lakeside Joondulup shopping centre. The morning was a mild 25 degrees Celsius, a gentle south easterly breeze wafted in from the Indian Ocean. As it meandered through the area, it seemed to stop for a second to plant its tender soft, sea-salty kisses on the faces of buildings, vegetation, vehicles and people outside the shopping centre.

Blayne and Sally had made plans, on their way to the Joondulup Blood Donation section of the Hospital, to stop by the food mall – grab a bite to eat and a drink. They walked through the portico of the shopping centre, past the cinema on the left. They cordially chatted as they walked casually along. As they took a left hand turn toward the food hall, Sally spotted Vampcirio window-shopping at a sports store to her left. He was oblivious of their close presence.

Vampcirio nodded, as though he were pleased at the sight of the sports shoes. He could do with a new pair of shoes in which to train the most recent casual basketball team he and the children's parents had put together.

Timmy, Luke and eight others – aged between seven and nine – made up two teams. They named the first amateur team Weststate Flare, the other team's name being Stateside Sizzle.

Sally stopped in her tracks, about half a metre away from the side view of Vampcirio.

'That's him.' She whispered in a shaky tone to Blayne.

'Well, here's your chance.' Blayne encouraged.

'I don't 'know.....' Vampcirio saw them at the corner of his eye, and turned around. He couldn't believe who he was seeing. Sally and Vampcirio approached each other with fragile caution, not that they were afraid of each other, rather they thought one or the other might disappear before their very sight.

Blayne stayed where he was, just in case Sally might require his support.

'H-hello Sally?' Vampcirio knew it was her, but couldn't believe it.

'Vampcirio, we were just about to....it's good to see you....won't you join us for a bite to eat?'

She felt small and foolish and wished that the floor would open up an swallow her. Vampcirio's heart dropped to his feet, as he glanced over to Blayne. Sally motioned to Blayne to join them.

'Blayne.' He extended his hand in greeting. His handsome chiselled face, his light brown, shaggy neck length hair, his pale green eyes. Vampcirio noted every inch of this extraordinary man, his lean physique, and his genuine, warm smile. *No wonder Sally fell for this guy.* He smiled, unsure of his feelings toward this guy, – Blayne – *Sally deserves the best – of everything* – he thought, and meant it.

'I'm Sally's friend, and colleague.' Blayne nodded in greeting. 'We're studying together.' He stressed *studying together.* 'I'll just wander on back to the car.' Blayne smiled, and nodded again. 'It was great to meet you mate.' He extended his hand once again to Vampcirio, in farewell.

'We-um-need to talk, Vampcirio.' Sally spoke serious, but quiet.

Terry, Tyla, William, and young Gerry flexed their wings, and soared farther north. They travelled west inland of the Gunbarrel Highway. They passed over numerous small dry lakes, and met up with the David Carnagie Road. They made their way further north/west inland of the Gary Highway. They took short breaks to catch a feed or two in the evenings.

They rested upon a gravel crevice during the daylight hours.

After days of sleeping, and nights of travelling, and feeding, Terry, Tyla, William, and Gerry arrived – exhausted – at a crevice on the north side of Nipper Pinnacle. The lads had travelled an approximate – and astonishing – 700 kilometres from Wanjarri National Park to Nipper Pinnacle.

The spinifex was parched, and wiry looking. 'I think I recall this place.' Gerry placed his thumb in the middle of his chin, his sudden enlightenment made him flap his other wing in excitement. Terry, Tyla, and William gazed around at their surroundings – they felt a mix of awe and trepidation – wonder struck by the landscape – curious about where THEY were. At least the lad has some notion of the location of his abode. Terry thought to himself.

'Although, I'm not exactly sure......Mamma!' Gerry exclaimed in delight at the sight of an adult female Gould's Wattle Bat.

'No. It's Aunty Clem.' She replied, as she zigzagged down toward the cauldron. 'We have been so worried about you, young Gerry. Thought you may have been someone's supper.' Aunty Clem squinted with suspicion, as she eyed Terry, Tyla, and William.

'These are my friends.' Gerry's chest puffed out with pride, when he introduced the trio to Aunty Clem.

The night sky was a clear indigo. A million stars winked – some clusters shot patterns of jet stream across the sky. The moon emitted her small, crescent waning light. A moon-beam reflected on Terry, Tyla, and William's vampirish incisors – their smile wide, cordial, but appearing a little beguiling. The trio leaned close to Aunty Clem, and devoured her suspicions.

Vulcarnau was still thriving. The Vulcarnoian community pogo-sticked along getting their day's work done. A small gathering of around half a dozen attended the Vulcarnoaumite coffin that Vampyx lay resting in. They sat around in quiet contemplation near the orange/yellow casket, usually three on the left side and three on the right side. They lit a large, thick white candle to pay their respects to Vampyx, and kept their vigil night and day. They could hear the soft, subtle drip of fluids from the cave's stalactites. The noise tiptoed around the cave, bouncing off the ancient ceiling and walls like a tinkling lullaby. They gazed at the coffin for around half an hour, as though willing the lid to open, and a regal, healthy Vampyx to awaken in the confine, step forth and greet them. They stared at each other with intense hope.

A giant stalactite above Vampyx's coffin chimed, oozing drops of fluid on top of the orange transparent lid – a silky sound of tinkling on glass. The Vulcarnoians were unaware Vampxz's spirit had left his coffin to accompany Vampcirio to attend the disaster on Planet Seventy-Seven. As far as they were aware, Vampxz whole body lay where he was twenty-four seven.

Blayne dallied along the west side of the Lakeside Joondalup Shopping centre, on his way out to the car he and Nurse Sally had arrived in. Sally walked with a swift gait to where Blayne was. She approached him, smiling.

'Blayne, Vampcirio and I have decided to have a heart to heart.' She tilted her head to the right, her sparkling blue eyes shinning.

'You take the car. Vampcirio will drive us back to his place.' She paused and rubbed her lips together like she was smoothing lipstick on her lips.

'Thank you for all you've done for me.'

'No problem.' Blayne nodded in approval. 'Call me if you need anything.' He turned and continued his walk to the exit of the shopping centre.

Acrobat's daughter, Gillian was seven weeks old. She had grown into a fine young girl. Her fur had become a pale grey, and her underbelly was a creamy ball of fluff. Her ears had stated to raise up, and balloon out as they grew longer. Her snout was transforming into a well-defined, strong anchor. Gillian was due to be taught to fly and hunt, as Acrobat had taught her son Jym.

The sun had set an hour or so ago, on the 20st of December, 2020, a week after yet another bushfire. The air was hot and dry, after a 32 degree Celsius day. The area was only in its infancy of recovery from the devastating bushfire, that took place in December 2020, that destroyed around 12.400 hectares of environment.

It was around eight pm. The weather had cooled slightly to around 28 degrees. Humidity was at 31%. A south east wind wafted through at 17 kilometres per hour. The stunted Jarrah trees waved their bare, charred heads in relief to the gentle breeze. Semiscorched tuart and eucalyptus trees appeared hot and bothered, their razed branches swayed slightly, as if they were drifting in and out of a semi-conscious slumber.

Mother and daughter stretched their wings and took flight north/east of the Cat's Eye Cave, into the Yanchep National Park.

They skimmed over and above the World War II concrete domed generator bunkers that were used at the time to protect the coast from enemy invasions. The bunkers had been recently given a face-lift, painted inside and out with tasteful World War II themes, and cheerful Australiana, much upgraded from the gaudy graffiti that glared outward from them beforehand. Set in a north-south direction, around 250 metres apart were these remnants.

The bushfire on December 14th 2020 had raged through the 2,799 hectare Yanchep National Park, destroying around ten hectares of bush, leaving that spot in charred disarray, but sparing the bunkers.

Mother and daughter had an exquisite aerial view of the Louis Edward Shapcott Ghost House ruins which the once Secretary of the Premier's office owned and used. The Ghost House was a single-story residence built out of limestone and red brick in the

1930s. To the south of the interior of the ruins stood a red brick fireplace with its chimney and badly deteriorated Metter's stove.

Acrobat went through the same drill as she had done with Jym and her many babies before. Gillian was a quick learner, catching three prey for the evening to fill her and Acrobat's bellies to the brim. A pale golden dawn was just beginning to be painted in the east sky, on the 22nd of December 2020. Baby Gillian returned to the Cat's Eye Cave – without her mother.

TEN

Dollops of pooled ruby, diamond, emerald, topaz, citrine and other precious gems merged together, twirled and swirled. They attracted particles of Crysythyst-like a magnet – from the devastated earth, along their streamline journey, to where they began to form a brand new structure. Lighshim and Lightsher's tears ceased to flow as they watched in amazement at the automatic and miraculous process.

The structure that faced north and quickly grew into a stark, glimmering tetrahedron with a thick, triangular base with four faces, six edges and four vertices. It appeared to consist of a solid silver metal, yet every five seconds it would transform its consistency to a different substance and colour, glinting and shimmering with each change. It had a heart beat, 60 beats per minute with orange, 120 beats per minute with red, 50 beats per minute with green and different beats per minute with other individual colours it displayed. When the edifice had reached seven metres tall, it stopped growing. The colour ceased to change – the final three being orange, red, and green shading into each other between their layers – the heart beats slowed to 70 beats per minute.

Another separate design began to form, in the south position, into a wide, stout dome, about two metres in width by round three metres in height, two metres away from the pyramid. It was made with what appeared to be a different substance, like transparent pale green crystal.

Another two metres in distance to the west, a couple of adjoining erect oblong shapes, each having two pairs of parallel sides and four right angles, but no equal sides, towered rapidly to five metres each.

In the east location a single erect trapezoid, with its flat closed shape, four straight sides with one pair of parallel sides, known as bases, grew three metres – base to top. This structure began as a watery pink and purple, then every seven minutes the pink and purple deepened its hues.

In the midst of the four establishments, with a distance of around a metre from them all, a fifth building was shaped into a long five metre rectangle, with a two metre square peak top. It congealed into a gold substance. Although the substance was pliable, it was sturdy. Its four one-metre by one-metre tall and wide rectangle windows faced north, south-east and west at the bottom arising upward, and faced the newly formed construction at their individual compass points. It had no glass, but dazzling rays emitted from the frame-less windows and reached out to the other four structures, bathing them in a glorious stream bath. As night fell, the rectangular square topped building glowed in the dark, as though it had strontium aluminate in its material.

'Our home is being transformed into an unknown environment.' Lightsher said to Lightshim, without looking at him.

'Yes.' Lightshim conceded. 'The buildings don't appear to be malevolent. I guess we'll just have to wait and see what happens.'

'Are there any occupants?' Lightshim worried.

Terry, Tyla, and William decided to make their temporary home high toward the top – on the south side – of Nipper Pinnacle, to where Gerry, Aunty Clem and their cauldron of Gould's Wattled Bats resided. The Pinnacle was covered with broken slabs of rock and boulders of all different sizes. They hung into a safe, secure red rock crevice, and slept throughout that day. A few days of slumbering and nights of hunting passed.

It was early evening and time to move on. Terry, Tyla and William thanked and fare-welled the cauldron of the Gould Wattled Bats who resided at Nipper Pinnacle.

'You take good care of yourself.' Terry stressed to young Gerry. Aunty Clem bowed her head slightly and looked forlorn, as she stood next to Gerry.

'And don't you go getting yourself lost.' William spoke with empathy. He gave Aunty Clem a touch of encouragement on her wing.

The three lads alighted and veered west-ward toward Gary Highway, then made their way north toward Windy Corner.

Their keen eyesight zoomed in on a bizarre-looking figure who was round six metres away from them. The thing seemed to be made of a greyish metal of some sort, with a strange shaped head, and squat, thick legs. It appeared to walk in a slow – staggering motion – toward the north of the Highway.

'What in gum is that!' Tyla squinted his eyes in disbelief. 'I don't know.' Said a surprised Terry.

'I think.....' William's voice trailed, when the thing turned around and raised its egg-beater arm up, and pointed it toward the lads.

'I think we better.....'

Dark clouds rolled, and rushed across the sky, speeding, darting in all directions – gobbling up azure air.Dry lightning slashed its razor swords – glinting, slicing – from the dense, grey, marshmallow cloud. Thunder creaked, cracked and the cloud's guts rumbled like they wanted to devour the earth. The dense, thick, forbidding figure appeared to produce a giant shadowy twin that decreased as its silhouette shrank with the changing shades of darkness from the low, murky clouds.

Huge, cool rain drops fell like a flood of tears, hitting the dry, burnt brown/orange earth, who at first declined to quench its thirst, then with a dry, parched thirst, drank up the rain water like it couldn't get enough of the stuff.

Martyz's whisk shot out a blinding, thin spark of Dynoetic that rose up and clashed with a bolt of lightning that caused an enormous atomic looking bright red-gold mushroom to appear where the two energies collided.

Outer light rays brushed the tip of the bat's wings, paralysing the three lads. They fell to the ground with a thud. Red-orange mud spattered around their bodies, from the dent they had made in the ground. Terry, Tyla, and William were shaken up. They re-gained their body functions a few seconds later, their wings took a little longer to recover. William acquired a mild sprain to his thumb, but no one was seriously injured.

Martyz crumbled to the ground in a heap, like recycled metal stacked in a junkyard. The boys watched in awe. Their eyes saw, but their minds couldn't comprehend what was happening to be real.

The storm had cleared as quickly as it had arrived.

'How's your thumb?' Tyla asked William.

'It's OK.' William replied, wiggling it. The chaps could use their wings after the scenario had vaporised. Everything appeared back to normal. 'We'd better get out of here.' William shivered.

At dawn, a brisk 17 degree Celsius light washed over Planet Seventy-Seven. There was no sun in the sky.

The light appeared to be dull, but from whence it came Lightshim and Lightsher had no idea.

The long five metre rectangle, with a two metre square peak top began to glow. Within a short time, the glow glared so bright that the structure's shape could not be defined. It was rotating, steady, drawing into itself, from the other four constructions, all colours the others' offered up. The structure threw out its absorbed contents through its square top.

Wispy rainbow colours magnetised together. They created a multi-hued vortex. The vortex spun faster. This caused the square structure on top of the rectangle to emit a golden orb within the vortex.

On the horizon of the east sky, a golden pin-prick size appeared. The coloured whirlpool shed its spinning vortex at a gradual pace until it spun down to a stop.

The light rose like sunrise, and grew, until it reached the size of a full sun – golden, bright, warm – nothing unusual about its appearance.

When the sun had been created, the structure reverted back to its original shape, like nothing had happened.

Before the sun had been created, the moon and the stars had functioned at their regular, usual status in the evening, since the magic moon cape had created them, but during day-time hours planet Seventy-Seven had remained in graveyard darkness – no moonlight, no sparkling stars – no light of any kind. There was no sound, with the exception of Lightsher and Lightshim's shivering terror from inside their restless gems shape. Lightsher and Lightshim could do little during the night. When the moon was in its full phase – the brightest light of the month was shed – it was not enough for them to go venturing out from their immediate environment.

Lightshim and Lightsher were familiar with their personal space, but they could not take the risk to go on an expedition. They were unaware how to, or where to begin, beyond their immediate vicinity. They did not wish to chance an encounter with any enemy – such as the Krai-Qtaur – who were maybe lurking somewhere out there.

Lightshim, and Lightsher were two entities with functioning whisk, but there could have been tens or hundreds – with functioning whisks – waiting to ambush them.

Lightshim and Lightsher considered themselves to be a little lucky that they had not encountered any Krai-Qtaur to date.

When the structures began to emerge from Lightshim and Lightsher's tears, they did consider the buildings to be that of the Krai-Qtaur, but then they discounted that theory. Lightsher and Lightshim were not Krai-Qtaur. How could anything Krai-Qtaurian be created from their tears? But then again, the other two reborn part Krai-Qataurian, part Seventy-Sevenite entities were created from the dilapidated Quixenuec – so were Lightshim and Lightsher. At least the sun was now shining, they gratefully thought.

Jym and Marnie had been away from the Cat's Eye Cave for three and a half months. When they bade farewell to Dogfeather, they had remained in the Yanchep National Park, some 1,000 hectares away, where they settled down within a gravel rock crevice. Jym had been away from Marnie for five months.

When Jym had returned Marnie proudly said: 'Meet your son, Jamieson.' Marnie introduced the two and a bit month old strapping young lad to his father. Jamieson stuck his tiny thumb out to greet his father. His wide, round eyes gleamed with delight. He grinned, showing his small, razor sharp vampirish fangs, two at the front top front of his mouth, and two at the bottom of the front of his mouth. His teeth gleamed as white as a polar bear.

Jamieson had shed most of his dark grey baby fur, and he looked like a healthy, juvenile ghost-bat. He was a powerful flyer, and astute at catching his prey.

Nurse Sally and Vampcirio spent most of their time in silence, as Vampcirio drove his VQ7 automobile at a steady pace toward his home in Yanchep, Western Australia.

Sally's face lit up with joy as they wound around the circular driveway. Vampcirio parked his sleek VQ7 sports car into the garage. They walked casually, side by side – not touching each other – up to the front door.

Vampcirio unlocked the front door, and stepped onto the hallway.

'Can I offer you a cup of tea, coffee?' He turned around to ask Sally.

'Yes please. Tea would be lovely.' Sally accepted with a smile. Vampcirio reciprocated the smile. His heart skipped happy beats, although he was a tad nervous. Sally was the first to venture into the kitchen.

'Vampcirio, you've had a kitchen makeover.' Sally rose her eyebrow in surprise, as she noted the radical, but tasteful, changes to the kitchen. Vampcirio raised his eyebrows in complex surprise, then looked around the kitchen, perplexed by what he saw. The display cabinets that displayed the sports gear, writing implements, and all the rest were gone. On the walls above where the display cabinets once stood, hung tastefully landscaped paintings, of the environment around Vampriciro's property and of the Yanchep National park, before, during and after the bushfires. The Crysythyst chairs were replaced with high backed jarrah chairs that had a flourish carved decoration on their backs.

It was like a magician had visited his home, while he was away that morning, and decided to wave his magic wand in one swift sweep – to clear away what was there – and make modern, current world changes to his kitchen. Vampcirio was anxious to check out the rest of his home. What changes have been made there – if any, and why? He offered Sally a chair instead, and went over to the bench to put the kettle on.

'Er-Um, Yes.' He tried to keep his composure. 'I had the place changed a little. A more modernised style was needed, I thought.' But he really didn't think so. He liked things the way they were. *'The Cat's Eye Cave.'* Thought Vampcirio. *'I wonder if that's still there.......My little friend Acrobat ....'* Sally could see the worried look on Vampcirio's face. 'It looks wonderful, Vampcirio.'

Sally gazed around the kitchen, and nodded with approval. Vampcirio vaguely smiled, his mind conjuring up all kinds of calamitous scenarios as to what lay in store for the rest of the house, but he was mostly concerned about the Cat's Eye Cave. He was more anxious about Acrobat.

Terry, Tyla, and William made their way back to the Yanchep National Park, from Nipper Pinnacle. They stopped at the same places on their way back as on their way there. They made a point to seek out the same tree hollow where they discovered Gerry. It was empty of any mammal life. A colony of ants trailed over the hollow carrying bits of food – some morsels larger than themselves – and followed each other in an almost straight line. Some slightly diverted from their line, stopped, and promptly got back on their trail.

'Phew! We finally made it home.' Tyla said, as he hung upside down on a rock crevice, waving his wings in delight.

'It's so good to be home.' Terry joined Tyla. Next William perched beside his two mates.

'Jym!' The three boys chirped in wonderment. Marnie, and their baby, Jamieson, flew up and settled down beside Jym.

'Hi Guys.' Jym thumb greeted his buddies.

'You wouldn't believe where we have been.' William gushed.

The Cat's Eye Cave was just beginning to open at the back of it to let out the mothers and their children out for the evening. Gillian whooshed through.

'Chirp! Chirp! Chirp! She shrilled in distress. 'Mother's gone.' She was shaking, as she held up Acrobat's left wing.

'What? How?' Kyla looked horrified at Acrobat's wing – all shimmering – all bloodied. Her little thumbs were curled up, withered-dead.

'We were going about our business-catching plenty to eat.' Gillian drew in a ragged breath. 'Mother dove down toward the ground to catch a lizard, then a large bird caught her. I managed to grab her wing, but that bird was pushing, and pulling in the opposite direction.' Gillian howled. 'Mother's wing tore away, and the bird flew away with her.' Gillian began to shudder; grief took over her, as she gasped. 'The Last thing Mother called out to me was: 'Fly little daughter. Fly for your life!'

With caution, Lightshim and Lightsher checked out the bizarre structures that stood erect, still, and looked like staunch overlords in their appearance. There were no inhabitants in any of them, but each building had been set up to be a home, with the exception of the mid-structure.

The mid structure was competely empty, and stood there in all of its towering beauty.

The constuction facing north had ancient Grecian furnishings. Two klines, with their woven base, wooden frame, and curved backrest, graced the left and right back corners of the room. The beds donned a woollen stuffed mattress, the covering made of linen.

The kline were adorned with seven rainbow-colored pillows. 28 fitted columns – 24 channeled –

erected around the outside of the structure stabilised the building.

The east abode contained Japanese contents. The space was set up in a simple way to create an atmosphere of serenity. The walls were painted in soothing beige, and milky pearl hues. Closed shelves contained crockery, and utensils.

A round chabudai table, with its four short legs, was in the centre of the room. Four zabuton cushions topped four zaisu legless chairs, each having a backrest. Tatami mats, woven from soft rush straw, adorned the floor of the all in one room. Two side-by-side futon, quilted cotton filled beds, were situated to the east wall.

The south building was set up with Baroque furnishings from the 17th century Europe. Dark wood paneling adorned the walls with their elaborate applied oak woodcarvings. The carved designs were cut out and pierced. The pierced block onlay had been adhered to a blank background that had been cut away. Some wood on-lays were created with a greater depth and applied to a lighter surface, which produced a dramatic effect. Cornices on the four corners of the ceiling displayed scrolls with bunches of grapes adhered under them.

A 17th century carved and gilded fleur-de-lis mirror faced the west wall. A wooden bed, with its intrinsic carved swirls and curls, was placed in the north position of the room – just a little away from the wall. The four balustrades were tall, and connected to the top and base, with retractable, heavy, burgundy fabric curtains – attached to the top posts – that could be undone to surround the bed at the time of the evening's sleep. Two geometrical wooden carved chests-of-drawers were placed either side of the bed. A coffer, with its pegged construction, moulded panel top, pinned hinges, carved panel front, and gilloche frieze-style supports was at the end of the bed.

The west structure was decked out with crysythyst furnishings. The abode had seven rooms, and was a replica of what Vampcirio's home was like. The seven inanimate objects that contained the sports equipment, writing implements, and the rest were displayed along the north wall of the kitchen. Lightshim and Lightsher could not believe what they saw.

'Has all this manifested through our tears?' They asked one another.

They chose this structure facing to be their current home.

ELEVEN

Sally saw Vampcirio was still worried about the changes to his abode.

'Vampcirio, your home truly does look beautiful.' She reaffirmed.

'Thank you.' Vampcirio tried to get his head around what had transpired in his home.

Vampcirio brought the teapot, and two of his best china cups and saucers over to what was a four-seater jarrah table where a simple cut lace table cloth was spread, in place of the previous seven-seater crysythyst table and chairs.

'What have you been doing with yourself since I last saw you, Sally? Vampcirio cleared his throat.

'I have commenced a medical degree at the University of Western Australia.' Sally dipped her head, her eyes moving back and forth. 'I'm sorry I didn't mention anything to you, Vampcirio. I was er- um well – I couldn't – I- I had to focus on my studies.' She blurted, raising her head, and looking him in the eye.

'I understand.' Replied Vampcirio, who had a look on his face that said he really didn't understand.

'And.' Sally continued, nervous, wringing her hands together. 'Well, er-I like you Vampcirio.' She teared up. 'And-well-I-well-I have never felt what I was feeling at the time. I suppose I got a little, well, er, um, scared-well – not that I was frightened of you – I just couldn't understand what was happening to me.' She placed her elbow on the table, palm up to her mandible. She appeared to be – in her mind – trying to string the words more clearly together. Vampcirio took a sip of his tea.

'I like you too, Sally.' He tilted his head toward her. 'To be honest, I more than like you.' He scraped his chair a little closer to her. 'I was devastated when you left. I thought you wanted to get away from me. Thought you found me repulsive. Thought I hurt you in some way. Thought-well-I thought all sorts of things.' Sally scraped her chair a little closer to Vampcirio:

'Vampcirio, I like your looks, your spirit, the way you think, talk-well-I love all of you.'

'Sally, I.....'

'Chirp, chirp, chirp!' The shrill, deafening noise broke their connection, as it wafted through to the kitchen. It was 7pm on Saturday evening. There was a ruckus going on in the Cat's Eye Cave. Sally appeared puzzled.

'Some dispute going on between the Ghost Bats in the cave.' Vampcirio reassured her, but he held a worried look.

'Chirp! Chirp! Chirp!' The noise grew louder, more urgent.

'Are they ok?' Sally asked.

'Please excuse me, I'll check what's happening there.' Sally nodded, as she sipped her tea.

Vampicirio grabbed his small torch from the bottom shelf of the kitchen cabinet. He raced up to the Cat's Eye Cave, bolted through the entrance, down the cave's paths, bumping into the occasional wall, and tripping over his feet. He was out of breath when he reached the seventh chamber. He saw a wing holding onto a Ghost Bat's wing.

'My little friends, what happened?' He sputtered. Gillian told Vampcirio what took place in the Yanchep National Park. She sobbed as she handed over Acrobat's wing to Vampcirio.

'Can you help?' Gillian pleaded. 'Please?

'I don't know that I can.' Tears streamed down Vampcirio's face. His face lit up a little. 'But, I know someone who may.'

Vampcirio held Acrobat's wing close to his chest protecting the scrap of his little friend. He slipped through the back door into the refurbished bathroom. The area was in the same location as it had always been, but the changes were simplified – brass taps in place of gold – porcelain sink, and bathtub instead of marble. He opened the vanity door, and took out a transparent medium-sized glass box. He placed Acrobat's wing inside the glass container – perfect fit – he closed the lid, and made his way back to the kitchen.

Lightsher and Lightshim had settled themselves comfortable peacefully, in what they named 'Our Crysythyst Home.' They slept together in the king-sized Crysythyst-framed bed, that was plain, but comfy. They made peace with their environment and made fun loving love. Every other time they merged together as one, a baby Seventy-Sevenite crept out of their oneness, from their top, bottom or midsection. The babies - a blob of pliable material - when they were first born. Their seven shape occurred ten minutes after their birth, their gems appeared randomly over their bodies within several days. Some Seventy-Seven children had lapis lazuli, jade, amethyst, some grew diamonds, rubies and emeralds. Each child was an individual, with unique personalities, and traits. Some did not make it.

'What shall we do?' Asked Vampcirio. 'I mean, about us?'

Sally clasped the outsides of her teacup for comfort, and took another sip of her tea. 'I know I can continue with my studies, and still have you in my life.' Sally drew in an anticipating breath.

'I know I can too.' Vampcirio replied.

'I mean, have you in my life, as well as do my own thing.' They looked each other in the eye, their faces drew closer, they kissed.

'I don't know what possessed me to *run away* from you Vampcirio.' Sally said, trying to catch her breath. 'I guess I just wanted to focus on my studies but...well... I just couldn't stop thinking of you – wanting to see you again...'

'That's in the past my love – I mean you *running away* from me, and me not having the guts to go after you.' Oh, *I'm stuffing up a lot of my words tonight* Vampcirio thought. The only thing he could do was – to kiss her again.

It was just after 8 pm.

'Would you like to stay?' Vampcirio asked, then thought that was a bit forward. There I go again. He blushed. 'There are seven bedrooms here.' He blushed deeper. 'I mean. I can make dinner for us.

'Yes.' Sally smiled. 'I would love to stay.... in any room.' She had a wicked look: 'We can make-er-dinner together.' Sally finished off.

Vampcirio and Sally slept in his double bedroom, in his king-size bed. He finally got the opportunity to savour her soft, silky, delicious neck. They talked, cuddled, and kissed, then fell asleep in each others arms – safe – secure – contented.

Lightshim and Lightsher had produced dozens of children over the past seven months. Some had grown fully to adults; some were juveniles, some toddlers, some blobs. None bore any resemblance to the Krai-Qtaur – whisk free. Only their parents sported the

Krai-Qtaur whisks – which on one hand were a damn nuisance – on the other the powerful Nueconiun energy the whisks held would come in handy – if they needed to protect themselves, and their young from any enemy.

A handful of babies had perished, for reasons unknown. These littlies were given a Seventy-Sevenite burial in various section of the land, within seven kilometres of the village. Although these precious gems were considered deceased – they were alive with colour, and shine. Over seven weeks, they had had sprouted shoots of a gem plant.

Over the following seven weeks some of these plants produced live petrified forest bark, then over seven month they grew into a stunning gem trees – branches of tiger eye, and sandstone – leaves of variegated shades of emerald The flower's stems were Amazonite, Peridot, and Venturine, their leaves of emeralds, and citrine. The plain-looking buds bloomed into exquisite rose, carnation, and chrysanthemum-like gem flowers.

The moon was full that night at Vampcirio's home. At 11.30 he got out of bed. He made his way up to the seventh room of the house. The door was plain wood.

It had no keyhole, but was not locked. Vampcirio walked over to the closet. The double glass doors were slidable. He looked in one side of the wardrobe, then the other – No star infested cape – no moon cape.

Vampcirio swept into the bathroom and retrieved the glass container that held Acrobat's wing. *'I guess I'll go to the same place where I met my Father when we tripped over to Planet Seventy Seven.'* He thought.

He held Acrobat's priceless contained wing high over his head, in two hands.

'Father, Father. I need your help.' He implored. No answer. Vampcirio concentrated more. 'Acrobat needs restoration.' He saw Acrobat as a whole, healthy Ghost Bat. Nothing. He put all his energy he could muster, and asked again: 'Please Father, I cannot do this on my own.'

Vampcirio was heartbroken. His tears streamed onto the container that held Acrobat's wing.

'What am I going to do without you my little friend?' He lamented as he half turned away. There was nothing he could do to bring Acrobat back to life.

'Vampcirio. Vampcirio.' He stopped in his tracks. A voice chimed through his mind.

'Father?' Vampcirio was unsure, as the voice was more softer, more high pitched than his father's. There was no image attached to the voice.

'My name is Makopska.' Her voice lulled. 'I'm Queen of planet Pyxic.'

Vampcirio blinked, twice. He hoped the voice was not a reaction to his grief.

'We cannot restore Acrobat into this life-time.' Makopska was empathetic, as she tried to explain. 'Her heart has evolved. She has chosen to carry on her growth in another realm.

Vampcirio was aware of the planets Pyxic and Vulcarnoau.

'Is Acrobat happy.' He sniffed back his tears.

'Yes, she is safe, and happy.' Makopska spoke with serenity, and sincerity, then she vanished in an instant.

Hot tears streamed down Vampcirio's face, and splashed, and ran down the clear glass container that held Acrobat's wing.

Sally watched him from behind a west placed eucalyptus tree trunk. She was unaware of Makopska speaking with Vampcirio, and she only heard scraps of Vampcirios' speech. *Why was he talking to himself?* She thought. *And what's that he was holding up in the air?* Vampcirio turned away east, then headed south toward his home. He went to the bathroom, and replaced Acrobat's contained wing back onto the vanity shelf. He did not see Sally.

TWELVE

The next day, Sunday, Lyle, Janie, Timmy, Lillian, and Luke were visiting for lunch. Before lunch there was to be basketball training with the Stateside Flare, and the Westate Sizzle.

Timmy was the point guard, for the Westate Flare. Luke was the power forward for the Stateside Sizzle. Vampcirio was coach for Westate Flare. Lyle was coach for Stateside Sizzle. The Flare were a more stronger team than the Sizzle, but the Sizzle were catching up fast, with their power forward gaining more strength, and agility over the previous weeks of training. The lads – and coaches – were serious about their game, but had fun playing as well.

They were gaining a reputation throughout the area. Parents, friends and relatives came to watch the vibrant matches that were held every Sunday afternoon at two pm.

On Sunday evening Vampcirio drove Sally back to her home in Nedlands. She was into her third year as a medical student and she had her quarter-year exams looming. After this year she would carry out her internship, while continuing on with her studies.

She invited Vampcirio in for refreshments, but he declined, as he knew Sally had a lot on her plate – with her exams coming up – and much study to be done beforehand.

'We'll catch up in a couple of weeks.' Sally kissed Vampcirio, and then bade each other farewell for the time being. She never mentioned she saw him performing his ritual the night before.

Vampcirio was elated when he arrived home – around 9pm. All was still, silent. He opened his front door, switched on the light, half expecting to see his home transformed again, it wasn't. He made his way to the bathroom. He wanted to pay his respects to Acrobat – what was left of her – which he decided to do every evening.

He opened the cabinet that held the clear container which encased Acrobat's wing, it was gone. Vampcirio shuffled over to the Cat's Eye cave, torch in hand. Terry, Tyla, William, Jym, Marnie, Bessie, and the cauldron had already left for the night. He scoured the Cat's Eye Caved in search for Acrobat's wing, half expecting to find all of her.

'It-she-must be here somewhere.' He muttered to himself, as he searched between the shawls, under the ledges, through the overhanging tree roots everywhere. No Acrobat's wing anywhere. He paced up and down the cave – down and up – then sat himself on the floor, palms of his hands cupped on his bent up knee caps, head on top of his hands.

'Chirp! Chirp!' The din woke Vampcirio, although he was not dead to the world, but had been in a hypnotic slumber all evening. The cauldron had arrived home – early dusk – from their night of frolicking, and foraging.

'Good morning, Vampcirio.' Jym hung upside down on the nearby ledge. 'It's pleasing to see you, early this morning?' Vampcirio stretched his stiff legs, yawned, stood up, and stretched out his arms. Jym, and Marnie perched up-side-down on one of his arms. Terry, and Tyla on the other. Bessie, and Terry perched on a shawl next to Vampcirio.

'Good morning my little friends.' Vampcirio blinked the semi sleep away. 'I know I am not usually here at this time of the morning.' He visited his bat friends early evening before they went about their evening business. 'I'm looking for Acrobat's wing. Thought she – her wing – might be here?' He gargled a cough.

'We haven't see Acrobat's wing since, well, you know – since that fateful day Gillian brought it to us.' Terry, and Bessie chirped, low, together. The rest of the cauldron nodded in grief.

'I had received a communication from Makopska, the Queen of Pyxic, who informed me Acrobat's heart had evolved.' Vampcirio conveyed to the cauldron.

'Where to?' Asked Jym, his wide lobed ears twitching in interest.

'I don't know.' Vampcirio frowned, and shrugged in bewilderment. 'I don't even know for sure if this Makopska was real. I asked my father to help reunite Acrobat – to us – when, instead of father's voice, Makopska's voice trailed through my mind. I was in deep grief, and unable to distinguish what was real, or what was perceived as being authentic.' Jym wrapped his right wing over his torso.

'I guess mother has left this planet, and gone to another more advanced place.'

'We can only hope so.' Vampcirio said, as he dipped his head in respect and grief.

Sally was in her final year of study. She had spent the last two years as an intern at the Joondalup Hospital. She had passed all her exams with flying colours.

Vampcirio, and her relationship had panned out over the past eighteen months, although they did not agree on everything they discussed – like general chit-chat – what to do today, etc. They agreed on keeping the environment, and its original inhabitants as natural as possible, beginning with their own backyards.

Sally had two cats who were well cared for and had their own spacious enclosure. Vampcirio was not all that keen on cats, but he admired Sally for being aware of cat's natural tendencies to catch birds, explore the neighbourhood, and be a nuisance to neighbours. He respected Sally for ensuring her cat's safety, as well as the safety of the wildlife in her area.

Sally had not moved into Vampcirios' home, nor he into hers. They spent their free time together between each other's homes, and both were happy with that arrangement.

Al and Lani had met Vampcirio several times. The first meeting was a tad tense, as Al was concerned for his daughter's safety, because of Vampcirio's unique appearance. Al didn't believe in Vampires – but had read stories, and saw movies about Count Dracula – before he met Vampcirio. Al had always thought horror stories were invented to frighten the wits out of those who were keen, and not so keen, on the terror tales. Al believed at his first meeting, Vampcirio was related to the 'Neck Nippers', or indeed was one. There was nothing sinister about this fellow, Al thought. And he was walking, and talking in daylight. Al felt ashamed of his assumption about Vampcirio. Vampcirio was aware of Al's initial feelings toward him – as he had experienced many an episode – but Vampcirio said nothing. He knew that Al had genuinely accepted him, when they could communicate on equal terms, as an equal human being.

The first official day of spring in the Southern Hemisphere – the 21st of September – Sally was preparing breakfast at Vampcirio's house for the both of them. The morning was a mild, sunny twenty-degrees celcius.

After breakfast Vampcirio asked Sally to take a walk with him down to the lake on his property. They had prepared a picnic basket full of goodies – sandwiches, drinks, and snacks – and a folded-up picnic blanket to take with them.

Birds welcomed the day with their cheery songs. The welcome swallow tweeted its throaty warble. The yellow rumped thornbill's high-pitched song wafted through the bushland. The grey currawong's ring, ring, ring, belled through the mix, and the rufous whister's do-de-dit conversations tuned into the bush orchestra. Lizards scuttled along dry tree stumps. Some black-gloved wallabies were still in their slumber, others lollygagged, grazing at their leisure. Some Western grey kangaroos lolled about soaking up the early morning sun, others hopped around – stopping at intervals – guarding their territory.

Vampcirio spread out the picnic blanket a little way from the edge of the lake on his property, and placed the picnic basket in the middle. He and Sally settled themselves down and gazed in wonder across the still, glass top of the water. A raft of Australian shell-ducks – their brown/orange chests puffed out, floated in harmony. The zebra-striped neck, and underbelly of buff-banded rails were striking as they grouped along the shore. The eurasian coot charcoal tails bobbed up and down with each dive they took. The Australian ibis, with its white feathers, and curved scribe like beak, foraged through the reeds.

'This is truly heaven on earth.' Sally said.

'Yes. This is a special place indeed.' Vampcirio spoke with a mischievous smile. Sally gave Vampcirio a questioning look.

'Let's get this party going.' Vampcirio unpacked the food from picnic basket. He retrieved a bottle of champagne. 'What's this.....' Vampcirio produced a small box from the organza gift bag he had in his trouser pocket. He stood up, and kneeled on one knee.

'Sally, will you marry me?' Vampcirio popped the lid of the box. An exquisite pink diamond engagement ring caught the light of the mid-morning sun.

'Yes. Yes. Yes.' Sally enthused, tears of joy welled in her eyes. She wrapped her arms around Vampcirio, he reciprocated. They kissed. All was well.

Vampcirio and Sally were invited for Sunday lunch at Sally's parent's home, Al and Lani. After a delicious meal and plenty of good conversation, they retired to the living room to relax over a glass of port. Lani brought in two glasses. Sally set down the other two. Lani went into the kitchen to bring the final two glasses of the 'after eating' treat.' Sally sat opposite of Vampcirio, Al, next to him. Vampcirio turned toward Al. Lani was half way back to the living room with the drinks, one in each hand.

'Al, I want to ask you for Sally's hand in marriage.' Lani rushed over to the two men, near spilling the glasses of port over Al. Al looked around the room like the place was jam-packed with people, he looked at Lani who had teared up with joy and looked at Sally who had gone over to stand with her mother, arm around her shoulder. Al stood up straight as an arrow, Vamcirio stood alike next to him. Al put out his hand to shake Vampcirio's. They shook hands.

'Son, you have my-our-full blessing.' He gazed toward Lani, who had moved closer with her daughter – to her husband – and future son-in-law.

'Absolutely, YES.' Lani spoke with resounding approval, and nodded like her head as to depart from her neck.

Vampcirio, and Sally decided to have a quiet engagement celebration – just with immediate family – as there was much planning to be done for their wedding, and plenty of celebration to be had at the time.

Terry, Tyla, Jym, William, Bessie, and Marnie – along with the twenty or so cauldron – heard about Vampcirio, and Sally's engagement, and up and coming wedding, which was to be in the autumn of the following year.

'We need to do something special for our human friends.' Bessie said.

'Yes we all agree.' The cauldron chirped in.

'It's still some time away.' Terry pointed out.

'But, that time will go like the wind.' William wrapped his wings around himself, wishing Acrobat was here with him. She would have some fantastic ideas. Marnie went over to William.

'We all miss her.' She whispered, as she wrapped one of her wings around William's wing. 'Vampcirio

and Sally's wedding will be held in the afternoon.'
Terry put his thumb up to his cheek in concern.

'We'll all be asleep, and miss it.' Said a disappointed William.

'We have a few months to work something out.' Said a positive Tyla.

'Yes, we'll cross that bridge when we come to it.' Bessie encouraged.

'Long before we tackle that bridge.' Jym was determined not to miss Vampcirio and Sally's wedding.

Westate Flare and Stateside Sizzle were at basketball practice on Vampcirio's property, at Yanchep, Western Australia.

Vampcirio had to extend his home stadium from a twenty-five-person capacity to a fifty-person capacity, as spectators were pouring in to see the basketball games.

A brand new girl's basketball team had been formed only a couple of weeks ago previously. A mother of a player had approached Vampcirio, and enquired about starting a girl's team. He agreed and so formed the Seven-Seven Sandgroper's girl's team, five players, and two reserves. Shila, a team player's mother suggested the name. Vampcirio was surprised – but tried not to show it by the name Shila, as the name reminded him of the events that took place in his previous dream. The girl's basketball team asked Vampcirio be their coach. The Seven-Seven Sandgropers' practiced with Stateside Sizzle and Weststate Flare, until another girl's team could be formed.

Westate Flare and Stateside Sizzle were playing at this moment. They were ten minutes into the fourth quarter.

'Go! Go! Go!' Vampcirio called out to Timmy who was dribbling the ball toward his team's hoop.

'Foul' Called Shila's mum Carol, who was a referee for this game. Timmy's opponent had stepped in front of Timmy. Timmy was at the three-point line, right in front of the hoop. He raised the basketball, and cupped it – aimed and got the points.

Westate Flare won the game, 32 to 27 points. Luke picked up his sports back-pack. He raised his eyes to look for his mother who had got up from her seat on the bench stadium, to go to her son. Luke locked eyes with a man – who was leaving the stadium – who wore a peaked cap, and sported sunglasses. The man half grinned at Luke. Luke waved, thinking he was a parent of one of his teammates. The man turned away and locked eyes with Lillian, Luke's mother, who was about three meters away from him.

'Neil?' Lillian asked. He gave her a crooked smile:

'He's done well, you've done well.' Neil whispered. Then he turned away, and rushed on toward the car park. Lillian went to go after him. At the same time Luke approached her.

'All ready to go home?' He was exhausted. Lillian looked to where the man had been rushing to. He was gone.

There had been much planning to do for Vampcirio and Sally's up and coming wedding. The eve of the wedding, twenty-seventh of March, twenty twenty-one had arrived as quick as the year had passed. Sally was at her parent's home in Fremantle, Western Australia.

Al, Sally's father – and two groomsmen, one being Blayne, best man being Lyle, stayed with Vampcirio the night before at his home. The flower girl, Lillie, and her pageboy brother, Ben, were with their Aunty Janie, and cousin Luke at their home in Yanchep.

The place was buzzing with her bridesmaids, all giggling, and drinking bubbly.

'I'm so nervous, that I don't think I'll sleep a wink tonight.' Sally enthused to her troupe.

'Us either.' replied the Matron Of Honor, Marion, as she topped up Sally's wine glass.

'Yes please.' Said Pat, one of Sally's bridesmaids, as she held out her three-quarter-drunk wine glass. No one was going anywhere that evening.

Saturday, 27th of March 2021. This was the big day. Vampcirio and Sally's wedding was to be held on Vampcirio's property, at Yanchep, Western Australia, down by the pristine lake here Vampcirio had proposed to Sally.

The morning was cool, but not cold, the day was anticipated to be a mild 21 degrees celsius. The wedding was to take place at three pm.

Sally's mother, matron of honor, and bridesmaids were fussing over Sally – mid morning – making sure her hair was in place, light make-up not smudged and simple, yet beautiful satin and lace wedding dress was fitted well. The morning's activities went by without a glitch.

The wedding party – with the exception of Vampcirio, his groomsmen, and best man Lyle – had made their way to his home in Fremantle where Sally and her party were all set to go.

The sleek silver stretch limo pulled in at Al and Lani's home to take Sally, and her party to Yanchep.

Sally was excited, yet nervous at the same time.

'I hope I don't forget my vows.' She said to all who were in the limo. 'I hope I can stand throughout the whole ceremony.' Chimed Marion, rubbing her forehead. 'Last night was a bit of a blast.'

'Yes.' Said Lani, giggling. 'Sally's last twenty four hours as a single woman.'

'You won't forget that now, will you Sally?' Said Marion.

'No, I won't forget the party we had.' They all laughed.

They arrived at their destination at 2.30 pm. The celebrant, Jaylene, greeted them with a cheery smile – then led them to one of the unoccupied rooms in Vampcirio's home, where they could all calm down as much as possible, before their short walk down to the lake.

The bridesmaids, best man, groomsmen and Vampcirio had taken their positions under the simple, yet beautiful, heptagon wedding frame. It was decorated with jasmine woven around the whole frame, bunches of Yanchep roses, and Yanchep bell-flowers were at the left and right corners of the frame. The mild perfume wafted around the surrounds – like a fresh sea breeze – in the mild afternoon sunshine.

Sally walked down to the lakeside, Al's arm linked with his daughter's. Al looked smart in his mid blue suit with a white open neck shirt. Sally looked stunning in her fitted satin midi wedding dress – with birds and flowers embroidered on the bodice, lace strapped sleeves. Her mid-heeled white shoes, with pretty diamante hearts embellished across the toes complemented her simple diamante tiara that was embellished with tiny hearts. She held a small pearl beaded clutch purse that contained a tiny bottle of perfume, tissues, and make-up mirror. The gold bracelet she wore had a single medium sized fresh water pearl that complimented her single pearl drop earrings. A lace choker topped off the whole outfit.

Bridesmaid's dresses were mauve satin chiffon ankle-length fitted dresses that flared from the waist down. Mother of the bride wore a mid-length light blue-silk chiffon dress, while the best man and groomsmen wore mid-blue suits with an open neck white shirt.

Lillie the flower girl walked in front of Sally while strewing pink rose petals in their wake, the skirt of her white lace ballerina dress embellished with tiny purple Yanchep bell flowers bobbed up and down. Vampcirio stood – nervous, yet elated – his back against the bride. He looked impressive in his mid blue suit, with an open collar white shirt.

As Sally walked toward Vampcirio and the celebrant, Vampcirio turned to look at his bride. Tears of joy welled in his eyes, but did not trickle down his cheeks. He smiled with pride, his vampirish incisors gleaming. Sally gave a shy, angelic smile back to her husband to be.

The couple stood next to each other, as they spoke their personalised vows.

'Sally Colston.
I love you with every fibre of my being.
From the first moment I met you,
I felt connected to your heart.

I will be there for you in times – happy and sad,
I give you space to grow in your own way.
You are my world, my twin soul.
Two hearts – one love.'

Vampcirio put the gold band, encrusted with two diamond hearts, on Sally's finger.

'Vampcirio Batt.
The universe has given you to me,
to love and care for all eternity.
Throughout our lives' ups and downs,
you can count on me to be around.
Our hearts are entwined, as our worlds unite,
this day we become husband and wife.'

Sally placed the plain gold band – with seven tiny engraved stars – on Vampcirio's finger.

'I now pronounce you husband and wife.' The celebrant smiled. 'You may now seal you commitments with a kiss.'

A cool breeze wafted through the area. Tiny snowflakes of glitter rained down upon Vampcirio, and Sally, and melted as it hit the ground.

Vampcirio, and Sally turned around. There outside the wedding party, and guests, stood a regal Vampyx. Next to him was Vivienne. Vampyx opened his cape. There on the right hand side hung Acrobat. She opened her beautiful, shining eyes, and winked toward Vampcirio and Sally, waving to them with both her perfect wings, then she shrouded her body with her wings, and went back to sleep. Vampyx smiled and nodded to his son and daughter-in-law, as did Vivienne. Then they vaporized into a thin, pale blue mist that became one with the pale blue clear sky.

'I saw them too.' Sally whispered to Vampcirio, as they gazed into each other's eyes, tears streaming down their faces.

The wedding reception was at 7 pm, in the first section of the Cat's Eye Cave. The cave was decorated with thousands of fairy lights, some shaped as hearts, others formed small stars.

The table was set up with fine crystal glassware and china crockery. Silver cutlery was placed in perfect order, white linen napkins were placed on the right hand side of where each guest were to be seated.

A stunning three-tier wedding cake – iced in white – the top tier decorated with a large single Yanchep rose, surrounded by a cluster of mauve Yanchep bell flowers, sat on a medium-sized, glazed oak table to the right of the wedding party table.

Toasts and messages were read out and the music began with the bridal waltz. Vampcirio and Sally looked like a couple that only had eyes for each other.

As the evening wore on – behind the party tables, on the cusp of the second section of the Cat's Eye Cave – 56 illuminated rainbow coloured gems came to light. They spelled out CONGRATS, as they sparkled, and appeared to be alive – winking, and floating to and fro – suspended in fresh air. Behind the gems were Jym, Marnie, Terry, Bessie, Kyla, Tyla, and William, bantering around and giggling in delight.

'We got to congratulate them after all.' Said an excited Jym, as he winked toward Lightsher, and Lightshim.

Back on planet Vulcarnoau, the stalactite above Vampyx's coffin broke, with the last of the erosion the drips had caused, and crashed on top of the lid. With a reverberating CRACK, the top of the coffin splayed an array of hairline fractures. In an instant, Vampyx opened his eyes, and stretched.

Invented words for Vampcirio story

Crysythyst: *(cris-ee-thist)* Gem found on Panet Seventy-Seven.

Cryx: *(crix)* Krai-Qtaur sargeant.

Diamise-Nuec: *(di-a-mees-nuke)* combined natural metal/mineral found on Planet Seventy-Seven.

Dogfeather: Barking Owl.

Dynoetic: *(dine-no-etic)* Brownish/red content of the Wajeta tree roots grown on Planet Krai-Qtaur. Used to suck up in their whisks, then be used as a weapon.

Fairsevenite: Planet Seventy-Seven's ruler.

Gemstarlea: *(gem-star-lee-a)* Seventy-Sevenites scientist and technician.

Golair: *(gol-air)* Krai-Qtaur inhabitants building material.

Jym: *(Jim)* Acrobat's son.

Krai-Qtaur: *(cray-quarter)* Renegade planet.

Krai-Qtaur: *(cray-quarter)* Inhabitants of Krai-Qtaur.

Kraiqtion: *(crake-te-on)* Planet Krai-Qtaur's atmosphere

Lightsher: *(lites-her)* Female Seventysenite.

Lightshim: *(Lites-him)* Male Seventysevenite.

Makopska: *(mac-cop-sca)* Female Pyxic Leader.

Makopsko: *(mac-cop-sco)* Male Pyxic Leader.

Martyxz: *(mart-tix)* Brother of Zymtz.

Nueconium: *(nuke-co-nee-um)* Combined nueclear/diamond processed blocks.

Pyxic: *(pix-ic)* Planet of healers.

Pyxico: *(pix-ic-o)* Inhabitants of Planet Pyxic.

Quixinuec: *(kwix-ee-nuke)* Combined processing plant.

Seventy-Seven: Planet of riches.
Seventy-Sevenites: *(seven-tee-seven-ites)* Inhabitants of Panet Seventy-Seven.

Shila: *(shil-ah)* Girl who transforms into bat in Vampcirio's dream.

Siliscope: *(sill-ee-scope)* The Krai-Qtaur army's telescope.

Toungaur: *(toon-gar)* The Krai-Qtaur king.

Tkobo: *(tik-co-bow)* Queen of Vulcarnau.

Treimix: *(tree-mix)* Xiantis's son.

Umberite: *(um-ber-ite)* Wajeta tree root substance.

Vulc: *(vulc)* Lava type therapeutic basin on Planet Vulcarnoau.

Vulcarnoian: *(Vulc-carn-ee-an)* Inhabitants of Planet Vulcarnoau.

Vulcarnoau: *(vul-car-nor)* Planet of the therapeutic Vulc, and planet of the living dead.

Vulcarnoaumite: *(vul-car-nor-mite)* Orange building and tomb encasing substance of the planet Vulc

Vampcirio: *(vamp-cee-ree-o)* Main character.

Vampyx: *(vamp-ics)* Vampcirio's father.

Wagjeta: *(wah-jet-a)* Trees that grow on Planet Krai Qtaur.

Xiantis: *(ex-an-tis)* Pyxic teacher of healing.

Zymeryc: *(zim-er-ic)* The Krai-Qtaur spacecraft.

Zymtz: *(zim-tiz)* Brother of Martyxz.

Authors Notes

I do not condone nor condemn alternative practices. It is up to each individual to do their own thorough research. Although UNCS it is practised, I have written about it for the purpose of this story.

The first birth of UNCS was reported in 2004, in Australia, I have moved the time backward to enhance the timing of my story.

Halloween is a complicated and absorbing subject. Many ancient – and modern – practices from around the world have been woven into the whole event, over millennia, up to the present. Since my novel is not a history about past and present Halloween practices, I have only given a glimpse of two past stories, one Celtic myth (Stingy Jack, aka jack-o'-lantern), and Samhain, the ancient Celtic harvest festival.

Useful Websites

Australian Museum:
australia.museum/learn/animals/bats/ghost-bat

Australian Government Department Of Health:
health.gov.au

Australian Red Cross:
redcross.org.au/perth

Perth Zoo:
perthzoo.wa.gov.au

Wikipedia:
wikipedia.org

Bibliography

Bays, Olivia, Seddon, Tony, Nuijsink, Cathelijne, *Japanese Style at Home,* Thames & Hudson, London, 2019.

Carminati, Marco, Zuffi, Stefano, *Borromeo Palace On Lake Maggiore, Masterpiece Of Itallian Baroque*, Mondadori Electra S.p.A., Milan, 2018.

Churchill, Sue, *Australian Bats,* Jacana Book, an imprint of Allen & Unwin, Crows Nest NSW, 2008.

Koizumi, Kazuko, *Traditional Japanese Furniture*, Kodansha International LTD, Tokyo, New York, San Francisco, 1986.

Lee, Sally, *A Short History Of Halloween*, Capstone Press, North Mankato, Minnesota, 2016.

Martin, Thomas*, Ancient Greece*, From Prehistoric to Hellenistic Times, Yale University Press, New Haven, London, 1996, 2013.

Nardo, Don, *Daily Life In Ancient Greece*, Raintree, an imprint of Capstone Global Library Limited, London, 2015.

Pearson, Anne, *Eyewitness Ancient Greece,* DK, London, New York, Melbourne, Delhi, 2014.

Richardson, Phil, *Bats,* The Natural History Museum, London, 2002.

Morton, Lisa, *Trick Or Treat: A History Of Halloween,* Reaktion Books, London, 2012.

Author: K A Worthington 2021